Lost Heart

Robin D. Owens

ISBN-13:
978-1530586301

ISBN-10:
1530586305

Cover Art

Dedication:

To All the Readers Who Love Celta

≈ Chapter 1 ≈

Druida City, Celta, 421 years after Colonization, End of Summer

"We have authorized a matchmaker session for you, Barton," Walker Clover stated.

Barton stared at his brother who seemed to have gone mad. Why was he talking about matchmakers? "This wasn't the reason I came to report to you," Barton said.

"Then why?"

"To inform you of my efforts to find Savi and Balansa." He hated to admit that he, the Chief of Security for the Clover Family, had failed. He'd misplaced two Family members, both too young to be out on their own. He felt the weight of *that* guilt.

"We're talking about you, right now." Walker's gaze remained serious, waiting as Barton's thoughts shot off in different directions. Did he discuss his failure or, even worse, comment on this matchmaker deal?

He stood stiff before Walker's regal desk in his equally imposing home office. Barton, and the whole Family of the prolific and skilled craftsman-decorators of Clover Fine Furniture, had all put their best efforts into making this room into the most impressive office in the city of Druida. That had been ten years ago when Walker had tested and risen from middle-class to the nobility. And taken the whole Family with him.

Silkeen wallpaper of a pale cream with a subtle pattern of four-leaf clovers was an elegant background for the mahogany furniture. The side walls held a few pics of Walker and their large—extraordinarily large for the colonists of Celta—Family. FirstFamily Lords and Ladies, the highest of the high, *had* been positively affected by this room, and Walker himself.

Walker continued, "The Family elders are concerned enough about you—as a highly placed member with a critical job and a public presence—that they've authorized a consultation with the matchmaker, GreatLord Saille T'Willow."

Barton sucked in a deep breath, suppressed his escalating irritation. "Such an appointment is too costly. Besides, I don't need a wife. I'm too busy for a wife. I want to focus on being the best Chief of Security for the Family. Concentrate on the Family. For instance, the missing Savi and Balansa." Savi was just seventeen, and his sister a young eleven.

Walker would someday be *the* most important man on the planet of Celta and that fact weighed on Barton. He couldn't afford to be less than perfect.

Walker waved a casual hand. "We'll get to Savi and Balansa."

"They are the priority here," Barton said, and continued as Walker inhaled to speak. "They went missing a full week ago!"

Walker's eyes narrowed, then he asked, "Barton, what day is it?"

His sneaky brother must be approaching the topic *he* wanted from another angle. Barton replied, "The twenty-fourth of Ivy."

Walker curled his fingers and waved them in a "more" gesture.

"A week after full moons. That's when Savi left, just before the ritual." Which Barton had attended along with many of the Family. "Balansa departed a few septhours later." Barton pressed his lips together. After Dark. A young girl had left the safety of their home, Clover Compound, to move through the city. No guards had reported her disappearance until he'd specifically asked. Another failure in his security procedures. Since then all egress and ingress was noted at the three entrances to the compound.

The strain of realizing a full week had passed seemed to set his muscles to concrete, his tendons like steel strands, too damned solid.

"Barton," Walker said too quietly, "it's Midweekend, and you are working."

"You are, too," Barton shot back.

Walker's brows rose. "Because I took the first two days of this week off."

Barton blinked, that seemed like months ago, all the days ran together.

"When was the last time you took a full day off, Barton?"

"Before this particular situation," he said, meeting Walker's gaze.

Dipping his head, Walker said, "I'm sure. Give me the date, Barton."

He couldn't.

After a full minute of silence, Walker said, "I believe I've proven my point. You work too much."

"I just said I wanted to concentrate on my career within the Family."

Walker picked up a writestick and fiddled with

it. "*You* are the priority here, Barton. Your life is out of balance. Everyone knows that. I've been giving this some thought. And I have consulted the elders." Walker smiled benignly, but Barton didn't buy that fake kindness. "And Mom pestered me until I gave in."

"Yip!" The slight bark came from the corner where Walker's Familiar Companion lay curled up on a thick, round pale green animal bed that complemented his red fox fur. *Barton smells sad and tense,* stated Argut, the FamFox. He added a yip of commiseration.

Walker scanned his Fam and Barton. "Smells sad, does he?"

Yes! a thump of the fox tail.

"He feels sad—" Walker slid his eyes toward Barton, probably studying their sibling bond. "Perhaps I should say disturbed, too." Then he faced Barton, tapping the writestick. Walker's scholarly face relaxed, but his gray-green eyes remained sharp. He wore his brown hair long, like many of the highest nobles did, tied back with a dark green leather string. Walker had even convinced Barton to wear *his* black hair long.

"You need a spouse, a lover, a partner," Walker said.

"Yeah, you sound just like Mom. I'm not getting married. I'm not ready yet. The Family is more important." He *must* continue to set the security procedures and standards in this first generation of nobility so they'd be *right* for centuries to come.

Walker stared at him. "You work too hard. You feel too responsible for all the Clovers—and we are many."

"I am the Chief of Security."

"And you have done an excellent job. So far." Walker's lips firmed and a line twisted between his brows. "You *need* balance in your life, Barton, and a lover and wife will bring you that. Keep you from breaking. You're the only one of our age group who hasn't found a partner."

"That's not true—" he began, thought about it, and realized it was. He scowled.

"Barton," Walker said patiently. "When was the last time you got laid?"

Barton really didn't want to calculate the number of those days, either.

"You haven't brought a woman to your house for two months."

Flinching, Barton said, "That can't be right."

"Mom knows."

Barton grit his teeth.

Walker laughed, a little too long for Barton's comfort. Barton didn't want to hear any more. He pivoted.

"You can go," Walker continued, "but the elders are waiting to talk to you in the courtyard."

Barton stayed, said, "Ambush."

"They're good at that, as I know."

A cackle came from the fox. Barton glared at him. Argut set his tail above his nose. *Elders ready to pounce on Barton like a fox on a mouse.*

"Thanks, Argut," Barton said.

'Welcome, the fox returned.

"I came to speak to you about Savi and Balansa," Barton said.

Walker placed the writestick down and scrutinized him. "You believe you've failed because Savi and Balansa left?"

"Yes."

"Barton, Savi is seventeen and just reached his adulthood—"

"He's still very green—"

Walker's brows raised. Not many people interrupted him anymore, and when he answered, he rolled right over Barton. "You're reacting to past errors of the Family and being overprotective. That Savi left the compound and the Family as soon as he could after he became an adult, isn't a surprise. He believes we didn't take care of his parents well enough when the plague came through." Walker's expression darkened. As a whole, and for living all together, each house abutting the next as they marched around three long blocks, the Family had been lucky when the horrible sickness had hit. But they'd lost people, mostly the elderly, and worse, the newest babies. Barton's stomach churned, pitching acid. That had been bad, fighting that sickness with their four Healers. At least he hadn't been responsible for that, a disease.

Responsible for everything else, though. He cleared his throat. "But Savi's eleven-year-old sister slipped out of the compound and hasn't been seen."

"No doubt she wants to be with her brother. She's a smart girl with good Flair, psychic power." Walker met Barton's eyes steadily. "Savi himself has good Flair and is intelligent. The children—" Walker cleared his throat. "That is to say, the *adult* Savi and his minor sister have a strong sibling bond. She would have been able to find him with that bond. And if she felt in trouble, she'd have contacted us."

Barton wanted to stalk the room. A fighter like he didn't show such lack of control. Instead he moved slightly to the balls of his feet, loose, ready for any attack. And didn't fool Walker.

"I want them back," Barton ground out. "They're Family."

"Savi is free to leave us." Walker looked too still. "And I believe that we should let Balansa be with her beloved brother instead of being technically legal and hauling her back to this Family."

"I want them back." Barton knew he sounded obsessive. Maybe he was. They'd failed the children before, he wanted to fix that. Ensure their safety. "The second-cuz closest in relationship to them and who has a weak bond with them, says they may have left Druida City. *Left the city!* Two child—youngsters—outside the best place for them."

"Clover Compound and Druida City, under your eye," Walker said dryly. He leaned back and tapped his fingers together giving Barton a smile he didn't trust. "And you think that you've changed the subject. You haven't. Your fixation on this matter reveals how lopsided your life has become." His mouth tightened and his eyes narrowed. He pointed his forefinger at Barton. "All right, since you insist of speaking of Savi and Balansa, we will discuss that, but I will continue to make my points with regard to your finding a bride and getting married. Doing your duty—your essential duty to marry and have children and love and live well—*that* duty to your Family." This time his gesture was that of a fencer ready to begin a match.

Barton's gut clenched. Unlike with swords, Walker won word duels with Barton all the time.

"Savi and Balansa have their inheritance from their parents." Walker named a significant figure.

"What!" Barton was glad the kid had money, gilt, but taking that showed how Savi felt the Family had failed him. "A good amount of gilt or not, he—they—shouldn't be on their own outside the Druida city walls. They are city child—" He stopped.

"When his parents died, two and a half years ago, Savi said nothing to any adult, but lived in their house at the far end of the compound and cared for his sister. *And our branch of the Family, the one most pledged to care for him, didn't pay attention.* Nor did he feel like he could inform us. *That* was the time of our deficiency, not now." Walker's expression became grim. "I think, at that point in his life, he had too much responsibility burdening his young shoulders." Walker's voice softened. "Rather like you. We don't want to lose you, too."

"You won't," Barton said.

"I know, because we will stop this hermit, too-immersed-in-work life of yours right now, before you break. A little too late, as we all agreed. We have let Savi and Balansa go, but we won't fail again. The rest of us are very glad that Savi has his sister with him. She's smart enough to understand, and tell him, that they're better off together than apart. Even when surrounded by Family. And she is old enough to share his cares."

"She's still a child! He's nearly one—"

But Walker didn't stop speaking. "Who shares

your life, Barton?"

Barton huffed, "The whole Family!"

Walker nodded. "You feel responsible for us."

"I am responsible for you and I must continue to search for Savi and Balansa, not mess around with matchmakers." Barton struggled to win the argument.

"No, you won't. Savi is an adult, Balansa is with him. They don't want the Family." Walker's eyes dampened and he looked away from Barton, then Walker tapped his heart. "I am the Head of the Household. My great Flair, psi power, is for interpersonal relationships. I have a bond with all my Family." He paused. "Including Savi and Balansa. I would know if they felt threatened or endangered, if they were sick or worse."

Another yip announced Argut's contribution before he spoke to their minds. *I looked for the kits, and told some of my friends their smells and we all looked but we didn't find.*

Barton nodded. "Thank you, Argut."

'Welcome. But we didn't find no puke or blood or smell hurt or anything, either. I told Walker!

That didn't reassure Barton.

Apparently it did Walker. "I sense they are *fine* Barton, give up the search for them."

"No."

Now Walker leaned back in his chair with a considering look. "You know this is an obsession, don't you? A too-responsible, guilt-ridden fixation. You should not feel responsible for the whole Family. Should not expect yourself to be perfect."

"I . . . just need to find them, make sure they're all

right."

"You want to bring them back to the Family."

Barton didn't answer.

"All right, a deal, I'll give you leave to look as long and as far for our lost ones as you like if you'll agree to the matchmaking appointment."

Barton stared at his brother. He wouldn't be budging. And Walker had said the parents and elders would pounce on Barton if he left. Nag even more. He forced out, "All right."

Walker snapped his fingers and a holographic calendar sphere appeared. "Your appointment with T'Willow is set for three days from now. It will be Saille's first appointment of the week. An in-depth evaluation that will last as long as necessary, perhaps all day."

"What did we have to pay for that?" Barton grumbled. "Extortionate, I'm thinking."

"No, he owes us a couple of favors."

Barton didn't know that.

"Saille is a professional, he won't take finding a good mate for you lightly."

"I understand." Barton glanced aside. "I don't have a HeartMate, a fated mate, like you, Walker." He didn't have the Flair, psi power, that Walker did, either. Mostly those with great Flair had HeartMates.

Walker said, "Cuz Trif and I have HeartMates, everyone else in the Family has spouses and partners and has married for love. You can't think of this Family and know that couples don't love each other. Saille will find someone for you."

"I don't—"

Walker snapped his fingers and the calendar

sphere pinged. "Workbell, the day of Mor, three days from now. Be there, or else."

≈ Chapter 2 ≈

New TwinMoons, A Week And A Day Later

Enata Licorice chanted the spell Words to open the oldest vault in the basement of the PublicLibrary —Secure Vault Prime. In a conference room above, her parents, the other FirstLevel Librarians, awaited the first generation copies of the satellite videos the colonist starship, *Nuada's Sword*, took as it landed on Celta. Those recordings had been made four centuries ago.

The large, thick, round steel door opened silently, and she hurried into the area that only accommodated two comfortably. Deep shelves surrounded her, and the general quiet of the library hushed into a silence where she could only hear the sound of her breathing and the rustle of her silkeen clothes as she moved. She climbed a rolling ladder to a cabinet, opened it with a four-couplet rhyming spell and two physical keys and pulled out the first copy of the spheres, leaving the original and four secondary copies.

She'd just reached the door with the small crate of spheres when a smell vault wafted to her nose at the same time an odd quality in the atmosphere impinged on her Flair.

Frowning, she turned around to scan all the familiar shapes in the dim light. She knew every volume, every box, every leather portfolio and thick papyrus envelope, every recordsphere and viz and memory sphere.

Directly ahead of her, on the far wall, she saw a

new book.

Shock ran through her. *A new book!* Thick, a good eighteen centimeters, bound in midnight blue with gold and silver flecks —no, sparkles. The spine *sparkled* in a random pattern, first a small gold starburst at the bottom, then a large silver one off to the left . . . mesmerizing enough to draw her to the shelf the book rested on. Above eye level for her, in the center of the shelf. Where she'd never have missed seeing it before.

An attractive fragrance came from it. Honeysuckle.

Bemused, she set the crate she held on the floor and stepped toward the shelf.

The closer she got the more wonderful the scent, not only honeysuckle but some fragrance that reminded her so much of seaspray that surf crashed and ebbed in her mind. She touched the spine and the sparks ran up and down her fingers to her wrist and back. She gasped, her hand hovered, but the surf and the scent and the riffling of her Flair kept her fingers moving forward until she gripped the book. The surf swept up her arm, across her shoulder, descended in a wave down her torso, nestled in her heart.

She drew the volume from the shelf, feeling the embedded anti-grav spell. On the front cover, picked out in silver and gold that gleamed real metal, was a map, the well-known peninsula where *Nuada's Sword* had landed, where the very city she stood in was located. But off the coast, outlined in gold, lay an island she'd never seen on any other map or ever heard of. Fascinating. More than fascinating, intriguing, arousing her curiosity as much as the book itself stimulated her Flair.

Smoothing her hand over the cover, opening it, increased the tingles coursing through her. Then the pages flipped fast and stopped at a holographic portrait of a man a little older than her with hair the color of her sister Glyssa's foxy red, though his green eyes appeared much like Enata's own. He smiled and looked so much like her father that she glanced down at the caption: Reglis Landu Licorice, CHOSEN, oldest child of Rhiza D'Licorice and Fasic Almond T'Licorice. Siblings: Enata Losa Licorice— *her!*—and Glyssa Nella Licorice.

She remembered her brother!

Enata dropped the book, but it stayed open in mid-air to the holo of her brother, Reglis.

Tentatively, she skittered a tiny step forward. The page flipped and the holo of the man turned into one of her whole Family, the PublicLibrarian Licorices. Her father with his arm around her mother's waist, his hand on Reglis' shoulder who stood in front of their parents. *He* had one arm around Enata, the other around Glyssa.

From their ages, the holo appeared no older than *earlier that year*.

Enata touched the book, and the page flicked back to her brother's portrait. He grinned.

Her mind burst as memories pounded into her and she reeled against the sturdy shelving on the left wall. Her knees gave way and she collapsed hard on her butt.

She remembered her big brother! All the times he'd irritated her or soothed her hurts or teased her.

Long conversations under the diamond star-bright night summer sky, and holding hands with him during rituals.

Enata clasped her fingers together. She recalled so well his energy passing through her, mingling with each member of their Family, enriching them all.

Tears flowed and she found herself making little wounded animal noises. How could she have forgotten her brother? How?

He'd been the heir to their mother, would have become T'Licorice, taking the male title of Head of the Household. In Enata's memory there had been a few months now and again when the heirship had bounced from her to Glyssa, then back again—a result of losing Reglis? And no one, *no one*, had made any reference to him. Neither her parents nor her sister. He must have vanished from their memories, too.

Chosen. What did that mean? It echoed in her mind like the surf, becoming so loud the word lost its shape and meaning, falling away to softness so all she heard was the "ssss" of waves.

She wanted to see that word again. *Chosen.*

The book yet floated above her head. She tried getting up, but fell back on her bruised bottom. Sniffling, she rolled to her hands and knees, then pushed to her feet. She blinked at the bobbing volume, trying to focus.

Feeling stiff, she read the events of her brother's life. Images flashed into her head.

FirstLevel Librarian, Enata Licorice, we are awaiting the recordspheres! her mother's voice, *the*

GrandLady D'Licorice, slapped telepathically into her mind, yanking her attention away from the floating book.

Enata caught her breath on a gasp, touched the volume. It sent a sizzling shock through her fingers, smacked shut, and whisked back to the shelf . . . and the sparks faded and an extra shroud of darkness descended over that particular shelf . . . and Enata recognized the standard books now front and center.

Enata Licorice, what is keeping you? demanded her mother mentally.

Enata hurried to the door, bent down to pick up the small wooden crate holding the vital spheres and pain stabbed through her head. Straightening slowly, she stood wobbling and dizzy, and her derriere hurt for some reason.

She scanned the vault. Everything was right and orderly.

Enata! shouted D'Licorice in her mind.

Enata sucked in air through her teeth. Despite her throbbing head, she decided to teleport to the pad nearest to the conference room. She hesitated. Something didn't seem right. She coughed at the dryness in her throat . . . but resolved to come back. Shutting the door, she set the security spells.

A couple of minutes later, D'Licorice frowned as Enata bustled into the conference room. "Thank you for retrieving the recordspheres," D'Licorice said in an icy tone.

After setting the small crate of spheres on the table, Enata nodded to her mother, her father, and the scry panel showing Captain Ruis Elder who looked in from the starship *Nuada's Sword*. With the touch of D'Licorice's fingers, the static image of the first recordsphere projected onto the long opposite wall—showing the peninsula Druida City perched on and the uninterrupted sea to the west.

"Enata, you look pale," stated her father, T'Licorice.

She put a hand to her head. The teleportation had nauseated her. "I'm sorry, I don't feel well." She'd been fine earlier in the day, but in addition to her headache, sick stomach, and hurt bottom, she felt generally ill.

"You may remove yourself from the Library for the rest of the day," D'Licorice said.

"Thank you." Instead of teleporting again, Enata walked down the ramps to the basement and through the tunnel from the PublicLibrary to D'Licorice Residence and up the steps to her bedroom. As she waved the windows thick and opaque, a stray stream of sunlight caught her fingernails. They glittered with silver and gold instead of being a natural tint. A very strange circumstance she'd think about later.

* * *

A Week And A Half Later

Enata had behaved poorly, and disliked herself.

The fact she hadn't slept the whole night through for fourteen days, since the beginning of the month, was no excuse. Nor that she *knew* something ate at her, but only recalled it now and then. An uneasiness seemed to live under her skin that she couldn't shake, part depression, part deep loneliness, part physical infirmity.

Her sister, Glyssa, had returned to the city, glowing with health and love. Glyssa had traveled across the continent and worked on the exciting project of the excavation of the starship, *Lugh's Spear*. And found her HeartMate. She hadn't, quite, fulfilled her career goals.

Enata had taken out her resentment at Glyssa's good fortune on her sister in a professional meeting before their parents, the other FirstLevel Librarians, challenged her competency.

Glyssa had responded with love and understanding and Enata had backed down.

A knock came on Enata's sitting room door. Glyssa. No, Enata didn't want to speak to her sister who fizzed with happiness. Tiredly, Enata tried to recall the last time she'd even been content—before her sister had left on her quest last month.

"I have hot cocoa, with white mousse and cocoa sprinkles just as you like!" Glyssa called.

Enata blinked, curiosity piqued. Hot cocoa on a summer's night, and a rich luxurious drink she didn't think any of the no-time food storage units bespelled cabinets—where meals and drinks stayed at the same temperature as they were when put in—had on hand. Hauling herself from her chair, she scuffed across to the door and opened it to her sister, who held two drinks.

A pang squeezed Enata. Glyssa always seemed closer to her friends than Enata herself, they rarely spent time together.

She inhaled deeply of the comforting scent, though it wasn't honeysuckle and that odd thought irritated. Where had it come from? Strangeness had invaded her life. One morning she'd found herself in bed with a foggy and dead recordsphere in her hand.

Meanwhile Glyssa stood at the threshold and Enata belatedly recalled that she'd gone to the attics the day after Glyssa had left for *Lugh's Spear,* and brought down new-to-her furniture to redecorate.

"Nice," Glyssa said.

Enata shrugged. "It had been more than a decade since I'd changed my rooms."

Glyssa nodded.

"Where did you get the cocoa? It's not accessible from any of the regular no-times until after Halloween," Enata said.

"I took it from the ritual no-time."

Enata felt her eyes widen at accessing a ritual no-time and taking food prepared for a rite on a whim. She'd never thought of doing that. Glyssa dared and carried through on her daring.

"That's not a good look for you," Glyssa admonished. She handed Enata the mug and it felt good on her sensitive palms.

Then Glyssa pushed open the door and glided to a wing chair upholstered in deep teal furrabeast leather. The color made her think of spring shading into the bolder colors of summer. A twinge tightened the muscles on her neck.

Glyssa said, "I've learned that enjoying the moment is important. The hot cocoa drink option in the ritual no-time was completely full. So we should use some."

That sounded reasonable. They were adults. Of course their parents could still disapprove and scold, or the intelligent house itself, D'Licorice Residence.

"Sounds right," Enata said. It took all her strength to stand up straight and pretend everything was fine. "What do you want?" She'd thought Glyssa would be with her HeartMate.

Glyssa lifted her brows and Enata rolled her eyes and sighed. Her tongue had tripped again. "Sorry for the rudeness," she said, and that came out more snotty than weary, too. Better she sounded rude rather than hurting. Picking up her feet carefully, Enata headed to a comfortchair.

"I have a plan," Glyssa said.

"Of course you do." Enata suppressed a sigh as she settled onto the chair. Now she thought about it, she'd awakened here a couple of times in the last fourteen days.

Sipping her cocoa, Glyssa said, "I think we should buy an appointment for you with the matchmaker, Saille T'Willow."

That had Enata gasping, "Such expense." But her heart began to beat hard.

"You're worth it. And you're the only one without a HeartMate this generation. You deserve that from the rest of us."

Oh, Lady and Lord! Could a matchmaker find Enata a good husband? Such hope pulsed through her. Hope . . . and fear, what if she didn't have a good match, either? Stupid sleeplessness, eroding her self confidence. She *could* have love in her life. "You think?"

"Yes, I do, and we can make a good case for our parents."

Enata's emotions wavered. "The expense!" They

were a frugal, scholarly Family, not putting much stock in wealth and status. They had to preserve the legacy they'd inherited. Should always be ready to fund the PublicLibrary themselves if the Councils failed. That had happened on Earth.

"Gilt is not as important as happiness," Glyssa said. "We all know that."

"Ye-es." Enata put her hand to her head, her mind spun and she felt such a mixture of emotions she couldn't speak.

"And it isn't as if the return won't be worth it. GreatLord T'Willow will find you a husband, a partner, a helpmeet. You'll be happier, your work will show that. We aren't meant to live alone."

Only drinking noises punctuated the silence. The luxury of cocoa with white mousse and sprinkles fully matched its decadent fragrance—and she tasted an added kick of mouth-heating liquor. Enata studied her sister who'd spoken of being happier with a partner. "You believe that."

"Yes, I do."

"It's easier to believe if you have a HeartMate." Enata believed *that*.

Glyssa said, "Perhaps. And I think we need to put it in the Licorice ResidenceLibrary database, that all individuals without HeartMates will be allowed an appointment with the T'Willow or D'Willow matchmaker, if they choose."

"I like that idea," Enata said.

"T'Willow has a ninety-eight percentile success rate with matching people, and usually the process takes from a month to a year. Just think, some man out there for whom you are perfect, is as alone and as lonely as you."

"No doubt HeartMates are matched quicker than the rest of us," Enata said, blinking away sudden tears. A year from now she could be wed! Meanwhile, she'd work on her emotional state and getting healthier.

She sat up straight. Set the alcohol laden drink aside. "Let's convince the parents."

≈ Chapter 3 ≈

Four Days Later

Enata sat, vibrating with nerves, on the way to GreatLord Saille T'Willow and her matchmaking appointment. The glider moved through the lush greenery of the high status noble estates. Her emotions swung from irritation at herself to hope to fear to . . .

Her parents and sister had HeartMates in this lifetime and she didn't.

That made her believe she was unworthy of such a gift, and inadequacy gnawed at her.

In a fit of exuberance and fear, Enata had invited her sister and her sister's HeartMate, Jace Bayrum, along to the appointment. Enata plucked at the sleeve of her formal gown of deep burgundy that complemented her auburn hair and the green embroidery the same shade of her eyes. She wanted to look perfect—worthy of a good match.

Then the glider pulled into the courtyard of T'Willow Residence and soon the three of them were admitted to the GreatLord's office. The left wall showed plants pressed against the glass of a conservatory, the other walls dark wood paneling. Each piece of furniture was a well-kept antique.

The GreatLord himself came toward her and the crucial nature of her appointment struck her. She stopped, frozen.

She'd met the GreatLord at rituals, a man slightly taller than standard, with chestnut hair and blue eyes. His fine features proclaimed him of the highest class.

He studied Glyssa and Jace. Enata turned and watched, but saw nothing unusual. Glyssa's hair was as rusty as her fox Fam's, and her eyes green like their mother's. Jace stood taller than T'Willow, with a leaner frame, hair dark brown with a touch of red. His narrow face held silver-gray eyes with a hint of wildness that made Enata wary.

Then GreatLord T'Willow took her cold fingers and led her to a cushioned comfortchair. She sensed a stream of professional reassurance from him. "Thank you for seeing me, GreatLord," Enata said.

T'Willow inclined his torso. "You are quite welcome." This time he smiled, also professionally, but looking as if she sincerely interested him. She let out a quiet breath.

With a wave of his hand, the thick arm of the chair sank, then the chair itself lowered.

She flinched but stayed standing.

His smile encouraged. "I promise you, this will be painless. As I told you and your relatives, from your background and Family history, I'm certain I can match you in the next few months."

With a nod, she squeezed his fingers, showing her confidence in him.

He straightened abruptly, reached out and took her other hand. Then his expression went impassive and his gaze distant. Great Flair radiated from him, sizzling uncomfortably through their linked hands, spreading through her in what felt like a net sifting and examining her. She flushed hot at being so intimately weighed.

An eternal moment passed before T'Willow dragged in a breath and released Enata's hands. She allowed herself one long shudder.

"My apologies for initiating the scanning spell so quickly without an interview," he said. "Please, take the chair."

Her knees had weakened and she felt fully as awful as every time she'd left Secure Vault Prime this month.

This fateful morning she'd surrendered to continual ill health and had taken a tonic the Healer had prescribed when Enata had gone in early for her annual health check. The potion had removed the last of the lingering headache, nausea, and muscle cramps. Now they'd returned.

She slipped into the chair and smoothed her gown around her, then linked her fingers and kept them close to her waist.

"Pardon me for a moment," the GreatLord said and crossed to his chair behind his centuries-old desk. He sat and turned toward the scryscreen inset into the paneled wall. "D'Licorice at the PublicLibrary, please." He shot a glance toward Enata. "That's where your parents will be, correct?"

"Yes," Enata said, her heart pulsing fast. Why would T'Willow want to speak to her parents? Could he not match her?

Clearing her throat, Enata said, "Neither of my parents had appointments outside the Library, though Father may be working at home."

"D'Licorice here." Their mother appeared in the screen. "T'Willow? Is everything all right?" Her gaze went past him. "Enata?"

Words rushed from Enata, "I don't know what's going on."

"I suggest you and your husband join us for the consultation," T'Willow said smoothly. "At once. Matchmaking at your level is always a Family matter."

Enata's mother's brows rose, then she smiled though tears showed in her eyes. "We'll be right there—" She stopped, swallowed her smile. "Enata? You permit?"

"Yes," Enata said in a small voice, still unsure what was happening.

"We'll be right there." D'Licorice signed off.

"Private screen and channel," T'Willow said. His hands waved in a pattern for a call to a Family that Enata didn't know.

"Glyssa?" Enata said plaintively, all her muscles tense. She wanted support.

Glyssa and Jace came over to flank Enata. She gave Glyssa one of her hands that Enata suspected might be clammy, then offered her other hand to Jace. Hesitantly, he enveloped it. "Thank you," she whispered. "Brother."

He flinched and Enata frowned. She'd thought he'd accepted her—them—better.

"Here," said a man's voice from the darkened scry screen. Enata frowned. She should know that voice. Almost . . .

"This is Saille T'Willow. I suggest you send your brother to me at T'Willow Residence immediately."

There was a long pause. "This is regarding his appointment three weeks ago?"

"Yes."

"He'll be right over," the man said. "Can I, or my parents come—"

"No," T'Willow said.

"Damn."

"Give me a septhour, maybe two before you scry me about results," T'Willow said.

"Maybe," the person grumbled. "Later." The sounds of a busy office faded. Who had a busy office?

"Brother," Enata whispered. She wasn't talking about Jace, but the man with a busy office who had a brother who'd met with the matchmaker three weeks ago. "What about my interview and ah . . . my evaluation?"

T'Willow rose, circled his desk and leaned back on it, giving her a brilliant smile. "As soon as I took your hand, I believed I knew a man who'd match you well. When I scanned you, I confirmed that. Your prospective husband is on his way here."

"Why all the secrecy?" Jace demanded, surprising Enata, but she liked that he asked the question she wanted to.

"It's best for the parties to be surprised, have no preconceptions that might come with a name," T'Willow said. He winked at her. "Such as those who believe the Licorices are archetypical librarians and scholars."

They *were* archetypical librarians and scholars.

"People don't realize we are *passionate* about our studies," Enata said.

T'Willow nodded. "Passion is a good thing to have in a relationship." He went to a no-time, pulled out a clear tube containing a dark blue fizzy drink. "Please drink this potion." He held it out to Enata.

"What does the potion do?" they all asked in unison.

T'Willow stood right before Enata, triumph radiating from him. When he looked at her, his eyes gentled. "This will make you emotionally more open and lets your natural inhibitions subside under . . . we'll say natural attraction, passion, love."

"Oh."

"The gentleman coming here will also receive a potion."

"All right." Enata released Glyssa's and Jace's hands and took the tube. She slowly brought it to her lips. Sparkling bubbles tickled her nose. She tipped a little of the liquid onto her tongue— sweet. One good breath, then she swallowed the drink. Effervescence slid down her throat, and her tongue swept froth from her lips. Already feeling a little dizzy and slightly hysterical with good cheer, she put the empty tube on the desk.

She felt *great!* Everything inside her loosened, all anxiety vanished, and she became aware of the intimate and pulsing bonds that linked her with her Family. She did love her Family. Every single one of them, even Glyssa's new HeartMate in a brotherly sort of way. She frowned but an errant sad thought escaped.

"GentleSir Bayrum, as a man not native to Druida City," T'Willow said. "Will you help me in this?"

Glyssa's HeartMate stared at Enata, then Glyssa, then T'Willow, his expression alive with curiosity. A good thing to have in a brother-in-law. "Yes."

"We'd recognize him?" Enata asked. Dozens of men's faces swam through her mind, from patrons she'd helped at the PublicLibrary, to those she'd stood next to during ritual circles at GreatCircle Temple, even all the way back to boys of her grovestudy days.

"You would probably recognize him." T'Willow gave her an impishly charming smile.

At that moment the housekeeper opened the door and Enata's parents came in, holding hands and radiating excitement.

"You have found the perfect match for my Enata!" Rhiza D'Licorice's tone lilted.

"That's right," T'Willow said.

"I'm not sure about this," Enata's father said.

"A father's prerogative. However, I think you will be pleased. If you would take one of the twoseats in the corner?" T'Willow indicated the seat on the opposite wall than the one Glyssa and Jace had returned to, far from the focal point of the desk and the two chairs before it.

"He'll—my—not my HeartMate." Enata bit her lip. "I don't have a HeartMate."

"No," T'Willow agreed. "But you have a man who complements you. Who will be a wonderful lover, partner and your love throughout your life."

"Truly?" Tears welled inside her like hope. "And discovered so quickly?"

"I promise you," T'Willow said. "But like all relationships, even HeartMate ones, this marriage will need tending and love and understanding. But I promise you that he is a good man and you can have a *wonderful* marriage."

"Oh." She swallowed. Love, real love. Someone who might put her at the center of his life . . . where she would place him.

The matchmaker continued, "I know him and his vibrations. I didn't know you, but when I took your hands I understood that you will be an exceptional match."

"Exceptional," said Enata's father.

"That's right."

"We want our daughter happy," said Enata's mother.

"And so she should be, as happy as any other extremely loving couple," T'Willow said.

He cocked his head and everyone fell silent. From the open window, Enata could hear a man stomping around, and using curse words that she'd only said in her head. Complementary to her?

"That man will make my daughter happy? Really?" T'Licorice asked.

"Get to your places." T'Willow put enough command in his voice to have Enata's Family taking their seats.

T'Willow opened the no-time potion storage unit and handed a large tube full of a frothy pink liquid to Jace Bayrum. "Give it to him and wait ten minutes."

* * *

Barton couldn't believe it! With a telepathic command, Walker had hauled him out of a training session for the bodyguards and sent him to T'Willow's. Made Barton take a waterfall and change into formal clothes of a conservative cut. Not that he couldn't fight in the Clover green tunic and trous, but the whole damn thing alarmed—no, *annoyed* him. Surely T'Willow hadn't found him a wife in three weeks. Couldn't happen.

And Barton had to sit in the back of a Family glider with a driver. Barton grumbled and swore all the way to the nobleman's. Glider doors didn't slam well, but he tried anyway. When he paused for breath, the housekeeper dressed in Willow red opened the door and waved him in, pointing toward a right hand corridor at the end of the entry hall. He nodded to her since his throat had dried as his guts twisted.

A man Barton had never seen stood before the office door. Tall, lean, looked even more common than Barton, which made Barton more inclined to like him. He stopped a pace from the guy. "Greetyou."

"Jace Bayrum." With a grin he offered a tube of sloshing, suspiciously pink liquid.

"Heard of you," Barton said, studying the guy. He'd come to Druida City from the excavation of *Lugh's Spear,* interesting situation. "What's that slop?"

"A potion GreatLord T'Willow wants you to drink to make you more receptive to love. Lust, too, I guess."

Barton scowled. "You can't make me drink that."

"Who wants to?" Jace waved toward the entryway. "You're free to go back to your . . . brother."

The guy knew Barton's sore spot, for sure. He showed his teeth, paced toward the nearest end of the hall that showed a door to a conservatory and back. "My brother's given me no peace. 'Get a wife. You want children, don't you?' he says. Nothing but nag, nag, nag." He ran his hands through his hair.

"The whole Family, nothing but nags. Wears on a man."

Jace sloshed the potion. "You gonna drink this or not?"

Barton saw milky pink bubbles rise to the top, break. He couldn't think of anything he wanted to do less. "There's a woman in there." He jerked his head toward the door to T'Willow's office.

"Three," Jace said affably.

"Three?" Relief surged through Barton. "I'm getting a choice? That's better." He stared at the drink, muttered an inward prayer to the Lord and Lady, manned up. "Gimme that." Barton swooped the potion from Jace, squeezed the tube open with ease, and gulped the pink contents.

Warm, and as frothy on the tongue and going down as it had looked, but . . . there came a tart aftertaste on his tongue, then an instant later the sweet taste of honey. A multi-layered woman? Women? Three?

His head spun a bit and he solidified his stance.

Jace Bayrum reached out and took Barton's wrist, tapped his timer. "Wait ten minutes and come in."

"Three women." Barton's tongue felt thick. "A choice, and T'Willow's supposed to be a good matchmaker."

"Ninety-eight percent success," Jace said.

Barton grunted and sweet honey fumes sent tendrils of relaxation into his brain. His tongue folded inward on another tart tang. "Not so bad." With careful steps he trod to a chair of wood and red velvet and sat. It groaned under his weight. "Beats being nagged to death."

Jace gestured to the housekeeper who'd come up to watch Barton. Obviously a Willow, he straightened from his slump.

"Ten minutes," she said.

"I heard the first time," Barton said.

With a motherly hand, she patted his shoulder. He felt the warmth of strong Flair.

Smiling, she said, "I know the procedure even though this doesn't happen often. It's exciting!"

"Uh-huh." Jace opened the door and slipped through, Barton levered himself up and craned to see, but inside the chamber Saille just gave him a smug smile. Barton frowned and began to pace again—carefully.

≈ Chapter 4 ≈

Enata had glimpsed a man, but he'd moved so fast! Or maybe her eyes had blurred. What she'd seen of him, she'd liked. Tall, muscular, he had a masculine grace about him. Actor? She could live with an actor. Dancer? She loved to dance. A man from the arts, how lovely!

"Jace, is Bar—is the man pacing?" T'Willow asked.

"Yes."

"Good, the potion will take effect sooner. How did you persuade him to drink the potion?"

"I told him that he could return to his brother, the nag."

Enata heard chuckles from everyone else in the room, but frowned. Her . . . man . . . had to be *nagged* to meet her? When she'd been overjoyed to have an appointment with GreatLord T'Willow to find her husband?

Only the continuing buoyancy from the potion kept her from shriveling inside that her match didn't truly want her.

T'Willow walked toward the door and tilted his head as if he could hear the man—yet swearing?—beyond the door, then strode back to the window. "I'm sure that his brother is already traveling here as a witness to confirm this match." He bowed to Enata's parents. "As you are. All of you, please remain still when the gentleman enters."

Enata slid her tongue over her dry lips, seemed to taste musk with the tiniest hint of sweet.

"Is Enata's prospective husband a gentleman?"

snapped her father.

"I told you I knew him, and I firmly believe you will be pleased," T'Willow stated.

"What are the ingredients in the potion?" asked Enata's mother.

Enata had some nags on her side of the Family, too. She smiled. If she and Glyssa hadn't nagged, provided research that an unwed Licorice turned angry and bitter, Enata wouldn't be here. But Licorices persevered until they found answers to their questions.

"What's in my potion?" T'Willow lifted his brows. "My professional secret. Nothing that will influence Enata against her will. Would you like a taste, D'Licorice? Any or all of you?"

"No!" Jace Bayrum exclaimed.

Glyssa sniffed loudly.

Enata's mother coughed. "Perhaps we can take samples home? For what this is costing?"

"Certainly." T'Willow moved toward his desk and tapped his scryscreen. "Mama," he said, "Please prepare some of the Recognition Potions for me." He aimed a smile at where Enata's mother must be sitting. "Two full tubes, one female and one male."

"Of course, Saille," a woman answered.

"Thank you."

The scryscreen pinged. "Here," said T'Willow.

A voice came. "I'm pulling into the courtyard, has the meeting between my brother and his match taken place yet?"

"No."

"Excellent. I will be there momentarily. I want to see him take the fall."

A thrill zipped through Enata, her breath came quickly. She couldn't wait with her back to the door, so she swung her chair around.

The door slammed open and her gaze fastened on the large and muscular male. Gorgeous man. Her blood hummed through her arteries and veins, heating her.

"Saille T'Willow, I hope you know what you're doing or I will beat your butt. I don't like being called in like a new guard." The man slapped his broad chest. "We've already had one consultation. I don't *want* another."

She had to stand.

His blue gaze went to her, did a quick scan and Enata drew herself into her best posture.

Then his stare met hers and Enata could *feel* the attraction weaving between them, fast and tight, an intense, colorful bond. Their breathing fell into rhythm. She grabbed the chair to steady herself as her mind dissolved into heated sparkles of attraction and drifted . . . towards him. Her blood pounded until other sound faded.

The very sight of him enflamed her senses.

Narrowing her gaze to *see* him through the haze draping her vision, tilting her head to feel his essence, she understood that they'd met before. But she couldn't place the setting. Not the library.

Another man came to the threshold, but Enata couldn't pull her stare away from the attractive hunk of male encompassing her vision.

Time passed, she didn't know how much, before she forced words from her throat. "I've seen you."

He nodded. "I know you. The librarian."

"Nice build," said Enata's mother. "But does he *read?*"

Still staring at Enata, her man smiled, causing her knees to weaken and she used the chair to keep her upright.

Then he quoted: "'Who ever loved that loved not at first sight?'"

Enata's father snorted. "A famous one line quote from the ancient Earthan, Shakespeare, that any man would know."

Without glancing at her father, Enata's lover softly recited:

> *"'Oh, she doth teach the torches to burn bright!*
> *It seems she hangs upon the cheek of night*
> *Like a rich jewel in an Ethiope's ear,*
> *Beauty too rich for use, for earth too dear.*
> *So shows a snowy dove trooping with crows*
> *As yonder lady o'er her fellows shows.*
> *The measure done, I'll watch her place of stand,*
> *And, touching hers, make blessèd my rude hand.*
> *Did my heart love till now? Forswear it, sight!*
> *For I ne'er saw true beauty till this night.'"*

She, beautiful? But his eyes had fired with glinting interest. She certainly thought him more beautiful and virile than any other man she'd seen.

"Well, well," said Enata's father. "More Shakespeare, from *Romeo and Juliet,* not auspicious."

"I promise, love, that we will not end as they

did," rumbled the man to Enata. He held out his arms and she could do nothing but run into them.

They closed around her and he swung her from her feet and whirled her. Pure joy swept through her at the romance of him.

Then he set her on her feet. "Oh," she said, clinging to him, loving the feel of his hard muscles against her. For the first time in her life, she felt more like a physical being than mental or spiritual.

"Oh, *yeah!*" he said and yanked her into his arms, lifted her off her feet, and kissed her.

His essence enveloped her as he held her easily. Big and tough was her man, wider and taller than she and that comforted her. She felt down to her marrow, down in her melting core, that he could and would protect her and any children they might have. Strong like bedrock, solid and honorable.

He teased the seam of her lips with his tongue and she opened her mouth to him, as she heatedly yearned to open her body to him. His tongue stroked hers and she returned the caress, sucking lightly to pull the taste of him into her, identify the components of him, each and every one that sang "lover" to her. But that particular cataloguing escaped her as her thoughts misted and blew away at the sensations he caused in her body.

The scent of him, man, musk, green growing plants deeply rooted in rich soil whirled in her head.

He aroused all her physical senses, and with that stirring, promised a fulfillment she'd never known.

She *experienced* much more of him—the aura of a physically powerful man, a healthy man who used his body as a tool—his Flair, not great, certainly not equal to hers, but with a resonance, a rightness to it. Yes, he complemented her in many ways, and she longed to explore fascinating differences between them.

Enata Losa Licorice! snapped her mother, shattering the moment.

He jerked, too, her man.

The man she thought she'd loved at first sight, as he had declared. Whose name she didn't know.

"Lord and Lady, Walker, stop the yelling in my head, already!" Enata's man said. He let her slide down his body and the feel of his thick, hard erection had her catching her breath and making her weak enough that she leaned against him. He took a pace away from her, and she stiffened her legs, but his arm didn't circle her waist. No, his hand curved over her bottom.

Facing her parents, and her sister and her HeartMate, and T'Willow, and another man as tall as her lover but with lighter hair and finer features, Enata struggled to control her breathing and an embarrassed flush. A full body flush, but thankfully only noticeable on her face.

The male newcomer, her lover's brother, began to laugh. "You've fallen hard and fast."

"Not funny, Walker."

"Oh. Yes," gasped Walker. "Yes. It. Is." He shook his head. "Lady and Lord, when I think of the nagging, the blackmail, the *deal* I had to make so you'd consult with Saille—"

Her mind clearing, her emotions settling, Enata stepped away from that large palm cupping her backside. He hadn't wanted her? "Is that so?" she asked, focusing her attention on the man called Walker.

Then she stifled a gasp as she recognized him. Walker Clover. The first noble Clover. He'd risen to GrandLord a decade ago, a man of incredible potential. Great nobles spoke of him as being the Captain of All the Councils someday—the most powerful man on the planet.

"Walker Clover, and his brother Barton Clover," Enata's mother breathed, her face shining. "With a Clover there is the prospect of many children."

Enata's father looked sour. "And they may be conceived right here before us. The guy had his hands on my daughter's derriere, and I know that glint in his eye."

Even more blood surged to Enata's cheeks. She glanced back at Barton whose gaze had fixed on her.

Barton stared at the woman before him, the only woman he'd seen when he'd walked into the room. His fighter's sense—and other senses, like smell—had told him two other women were in the room. He also knew that three men impinged on his space when he'd entered: Saille T'Willow, friend; the adventurer and an older man. None of them could take him.

Now Walker had pushed Barton into trouble with his less-than-smooth words, making it sound like he didn't want his lady. Dammit!

Barton's beloved stared at him with anger and hurt in her eyes. The bond between them that had been so open and warm—*hot* with pleasurable sensation—constricted. Her admiration of his form, her delight in his poetry, and her gratitude at having a wonderful match—those feelings slowed. Because he hadn't wanted a woman in the past, had fought the matchmaking.

He sidled a half-pace toward her, gave her his most winning smile, the one showing the crease in his left cheek.

With his most sincere look, one that came from his heart, he said, "I had my doubts. Before I met you." Reaching out, he grasped her hand. Oh, yeah! That crackle of energy between them triggered more aching desire. Made him want something more than sex, true *bonding* with this one woman. He needed her, now. Needed to be in her now, especially since she'd drawn away from him.

He scanned the room, spotted the long couch. Another pace and he had his arm around Enata's waist and quickening passion filled him. Her body became supple under his arm and she moved with him as they danced, touching, retreating, touching longer and harder, toward the fulfillment of desire.

That couch looked exactly right. He drew her in that direction.

Saille Willow stepped in front of him with raised brows and a smirk. "Your brother is here. And Enata may wish to introduce you to her Family."

Barton jerked to a stop. Brother. Walker. Barton could take Walker, lay him out and Saille, too, just as long as he got to that couch with his lady.

But she'd stiffened and a curse rose in his brain.

Family, the word whispered from her mind to his. He vaguely recalled that not only Walker and Saille were here, but a couple of females. Who, though he'd like to get rid of, he couldn't actually force to leave. And that would take time and break this wonderful spell he tightly held on to.

"Barton!" Walker's tone of command, which Barton ignored. Saille T'Willow stayed in front of him. Hell. Didn't sound like he and his woman were getting horizontal on that couch.

"Enata!" Another command tone in an older female noble accent and the last of the pliancy of his lady in his arms vanished.

He looked down at her, squeezed her waist. The more he touched her, the more he liked it. From the feedback through their newly formed bond, the more she wanted him to keep his hands on her. He could do that. He liked how their link expanded, strengthened, tightened, settling deeper into both of them, the longer they connected physically.

But she was ready to step away and others circled around him, blocking him, them, from the couch.

≈ Chapter 5 ≈

With a thump of breath exiting his lungs, Barton relinquished the immediate satisfaction of sex and began to think. As lust fog cleared, one name anchored into his brain. "Enata?" he asked.

She reacted to her name on his lips, shivered with heightened sexuality. Too damn bad they weren't alone. She shifted from foot to foot, a bad habit. Yeah, unfortunately he was thinking again.

"Enata Licorice, FirstLevel Librarian," she said, her wide pupils showed against emerald.

"A name as beautiful as you." Still holding her, he gave her a half-bow. "Barton Clover, your future husband."

"Chief of Security for the Clover Family," Walker said.

A spark of knowledge in her brain filtered to Barton—*Chief of Security, fighter, explains muscularity, graceful movement, complete manliness.*

He grinned, really wished the room was only theirs. Especially when an older man, obviously a nobleman and Enata's father, took the match-maker's place in front of them.

"Greetyou, Barton Clover." T'Licorice bowed, and his bow said a lot of things. He was an older GrandLord acknowledging a younger man. And that younger man, Barton, was brother to a GrandLord but did not have a title himself.

"Papa!" Enata scolded, so Barton got the idea that T'Licorice didn't usually act so formally.

Evidently the guy didn't like him. Probably

thought he and Enata moved too fast. This *was* a matchmaker's office, and they'd brought their daughter in. What had they expected? And nothing and nobody's opinion and actions except Enata's would stop Barton from being with her, claiming her, sweeping her off to his house.

But his neck burned in embarrassment that his standard quick thoughts had mired in passion, and his physical reflexes stalled. He returned the bow. "Greetyou, T'Licorice." Reluctantly he slipped his arm from Enata's waist to grasp her fingers and make a deeper bow to Enata's mother who he recognized as the holder of the Licorice title. "Greetyou, D'Licorice." Enata appeared to take after her mother more than her father in coloring and manner. A stiffer, more logical, less affectionate woman. Give Barton and the Clovers a few weeks and she'd loosen up.

"Hey, brother." Walker buffeted Barton on his shoulder, leaned down and kissed Enata's cheek. "Welcome to the Clover Family, Enata Licorice. Call me Walker."

So *now* Walker went all smooth, but he also spread an aura of approval and satisfaction that encompassed them all. Most of them smiled. Not to mention Walker streamed warmth and affection and excitement from the whole Clover Family because Barton had found his wife.

That had Enata relaxing, sensing through her bond with Barton all the love that bound his Family together.

Walker glanced around at everyone, paying more attention to them than Barton. His focus remained on his Enata. "All of you, call me Walker, it's easier."

"A spouse found for my Enata so quickly," plainted Enata's mother.

Barton wouldn't let the tiniest objection stand. He angled toward Enata, and his gaze caught on the beauty of her again, the narrow face with big deep emerald eyes, the red-auburn hair, her elegant, supple body. Her intelligence and honor. Yes, he sensed those, too.

He sent his wonder at the whole of her along their link, rubbed his chest. "You're here. You're just here, already in my heart. It only needed seeing you."

She blinked away tears. He understood the emotions she received from him through their instant bond filled her, easing some inner loneliness and emotional ache. He squeezed her fingers, still linked with his as their other connections continued to develop.

"I think the potion had something to do with having Barton fall in love with Enata immediately," Jace Bayrum, the adventurer, muttered. Barton hadn't forgotten the guy was in the room, but had discounted him. Barton swung around to snap at him and stopped at the sight of people standing in the hallway. A couple wore Willow livery, but he swallowed as he saw his parents. Either Walker had brought them or they'd heard the news and come on their own. Dammit.

They beamed love and pride at him, though his mother wept. He'd be the last of her five children to marry. He winced inwardly at the pain he'd caused her. Done now.

Enata had turned with him and she gave a little gasp. *Your parents! What if they don't like me?*

He heard her mental voice clearly and tightened his grip on her fingers. *Like my brother, they already accept you as part of the Family.* He paused, glad he could speak with her telepathically so quickly and easily. *Now, on the other hand, your folks don't like me too much.*

Papa? Mama? he heard her send to her parents . . . so Barton and she were that close already . . . if he didn't love her so much, he'd be wary. Especially since he'd begun to link with the rest of her Family.

The older man's face relaxed into more amiable lines. He offered his hand. "Welcome to the Licorice Family, Barton Clover. Enata is our heir. She will be D'Licorice one day. Should you wish to live with us, our Residence is available."

T'Licorice continued to poke at Barton. He was the Chief of Security, and had to live in the Clover Compound.

And, yeah, the Clovers had the unique Compound, row houses around three blocks, all accessed from the courtyards, *but* the Licorices had an intelligent Residence. An intelligent house spoke of the Family's longevity. Barton thought the PublicLibrary was self-aware, too. It'd be another hundred and fifty years before the original Clover house could think for itself.

"You can be the Licorice Head of Security," D'Licorice offered and Barton didn't know whether she was being snide or not.

He coughed gently. "I have my own personal

house in the Clover Compound."

Enata glanced up at him, brows down. "A whole house? For yourself only?"

Swinging her and catching her other hand, he smiled down at her. "For you, too, and our children."

Her eyes glazed a little.

"There are plenty of Clovers. We don't have to start our own personal family too soon. Plenty of time for loving before children."

"I . . . that sounds wonderful," she whispered.

Barton began to feel more in charge. He dropped her hands, set his arm around her waist, picked her up and set her so their sides touched and they faced her parents, couple to couple. He met their eyes, nodded to them both. "And there are how many of you?"

"Four," T'Licorice said.

"Four," Barton said flatly. He pivoted in place and looked at every member of her Family. "There are nearly two hundred Clovers." He glanced at Walker who just raised his brows, like he expected Barton to deal with the living arrangements situation.

A very touchy conversation that affected Enata's future, his future, the future of both Families. "The numbers of my Family make my responsibility to them weighty." And the images of Savi and Balansa, who'd he'd continued to look for, and whose disappearance still haunted him, rose to his mind.

Enata wrapped her arm around his waist, sent him comfort through their connection.

"I need to be at the Clover Compound for now." He looked down at Enata. Yes, she *would* be a helpmeet and a partner. "My lady must stay with us, too."

"I agree." Enata stuck her chin out. "For the first month perhaps. Then we can consider alternating our living arrangements. Like many other noble homes built soon after colonization, D'Licorice Residence has plenty of space," she said aloud. Privately, and not looking at him, she said, *Living with only you is an odd notion. I've always lived with my Family.*

He replied mentally, *I lived in my parents' house until I chose my own and we finished it. There are several new homes if you would prefer a different area.* He didn't care for that idea since he'd chosen his house for the best placement to oversee the security of the Family, particularly Walker. *Or you—WE—can redecorate my—OUR—home.* As her mind shadowed with doubt, he grasped for a lure. *You know my cuz is the best interior designer in Druida City. I've saved my gilt, spend whatever you want.*

She sniffed. *We are not a profligate Family.*

You must feel at home in my house, he sent. Intelligent Licorice house or not, he wasn't going to spend a lot of time there. Would *not* move into rooms there. The Clover Compound was his home and responsibility and he wouldn't give that up.

"Enata is my heir," her mother repeated and Barton got emotions from D'Licorice through her bond with her daughter. D'Licorice felt a near desperate fear of loss, a determination to fight anyone and everyone for her child, for the PublicLibrary legacy. And she felt great pride in Enata that wrenched at his love's soft heart.

Barton's gaze arrowed toward the sister standing with her HeartMate by the door. He said, "You have another child."

"You have *many* other guards," D'Licorice snapped back.

"I like my job," Barton said.

"I do too," Enata said. She straightened tall beside him. "We Licorices have a duty to the people of Druida City, to Celta itself."

Oh, yeah, he *experienced* that complete dedication from her.

He and Walker grunted at the same time, acknowledging the point.

Mixed loyalties. Barton gritted his teeth. They *could* work through that. Conflicting loyalties that tore them from inside and out would be more difficult.

The sister—Glyssa?—pronounced, "I cannot become D'Licorice. I will not be remaining in Druida. The community at the excavation of *Lugh's Spear* calls us."

Enata stared at her sister, believing her. Now that she'd focused on something other than her developing bond with Barton, she could sense all the other ties to her in the room. Her sister no longer considered Druida City her primary home, and Jace Bayrum, Glyssa's HeartMate, definitely wanted to be on the eastern frontier.

Which meant Enata *would* be the future D'Licorice, a title that had never, quite, felt within her grasp.

Walker Clover's aura seemed to expand throughout the room, touching them all. And Enata understood another essential fact. Walker, Barton, and the whole Clover Family had the ultimate goal of ensuring Walker became Captain of AllCouncils.

Enata's ultimate goal was different. Like every librarian on the planet, she was charged with preserving information for their descendants. Those goals might not be mutually exclusive, but she would *not* relinquish the primary objective of her life.

She felt a welling of . . . *love* . . . could it truly be love so quickly, at first sight? . . . from Barton. He dropped a kiss on her head.

Yes, the more they touched, the more concrete the bond set between them and the deeper the link sank into her inner self.

Still emanating authority, Walker said, "We can work all this out later. I'm sure *some* of our Family would like to apprentice themselves to you—and when Barton and Enata have children, you might choose one to follow you rather than Enata." Walker spread his hands. "The options are many."

"Yes, this can all be worked out later. Now we should celebrate an excellent match!" said the Willow housekeeper from the doorway. She brought in a tray of fizz-wine and flutes. The older Clover couple (who must be Barton's parents because he looked a little like both of them) scrutinized Enata, then beamed at her.

The Willow housekeeper poured the drinks and passed them around.

"To Barton and Enata!" T'Willow, the matchmaker, toasted.

A great wave of good wishes washed over her, through her, and Barton, too. Enata swallowed tears.

Everyone drank. Naturally the fizz-wine was top-of-the-pyramid. Since she still experienced a giddiness from the blue potion she'd drunk, Enata took only a sip.

This event had wrenched her life—her Family's lives—into changes she hadn't imagined, and so very rapidly. When she'd hoped GreatLord T'Willow would find her a match, she'd gauged that would happen from a month to a year, or longer. Not a few minutes after she'd arrived for the appointment. She glanced at the wall timer, less than seventy minutes, a septhour, had transpired since she'd walked through the door!

So very much change. The Licorices, in general, didn't roll very quickly or gracefully with great change.

After they drank, T'Willow bowed to Glyssa, then the older Licorices. "I believe you have a connection with GreatCircle Temple?" he asked.

"Yes," Glyssa replied. "My friend, Tiana Mugwort, is a priestess at GreatCircle Temple."

"You might scry her to arrange a wedding—" T'Willow began.

"Good, the marriage ritual can be tonight." In a quick move and with easy strength, Barton scooped Enata into his arms. Her nearly-full glass tilted and splashed down his chest and onto the thick Chinju rug.

Everyone laughed and Enata flushed again. Some of the heat on her cheeks even came from embarrassment. Mostly, being held and enveloped by Barton had desire surging through her body. She wanted those big hands running along her bare skin.

Barton said a couplet and his shirt warmed and dried beneath her. Walker took her glass and set it aside.

"A wedding ritual tonight!" her father protested, frowning at Barton holding Enata. "Usually engaged couples wait for a while—"

"No reason to wait, is there?" T'Willow asked gently. "The match is exceptional, the pair ready to bond, and the Clovers act expeditiously. I'm sure both Families have very efficient ladies who can organize—"

"The women—" Walker and Barton said together. They almost shuddered in unison, too. Enata felt the ripple of Barton's body against her. Nice muscles. Then she saw the jut of his chin. "I want to be married tonight. We *do* have a lot of women who can organize this."

"I must scry Tiana Mugwort," Glyssa said faintly.

"For sure," Barton said. He smiled with glee at Walker. "You alert the Clover women, Head of the Household. Make it happen."

"Yes, and you alert all the guards who will be needed tonight at GreatCircle Temple, providing we *get* that venue," Walker shot back.

Barton shook his head. "Nope, *you*, Head-of-the-Household-who-set-this-all-up-for-my-own-good, contact my second in command. I'm not working today. I have another major priority. One that you wished for me." He jiggled Enata a little.

Kissing her temple, he said, "Say good-bye to your Family." He grinned, but she felt a blazing heat through their bond, a red haze of desire that had her sex dampening. "We have a personal link to cement."

"No." Walker Clover walked up to stand close before them. "If you want a good Marriage Ritual tonight—

"Simple ritual," Barton muttered. "Make it short, not a dam—not a three septhour ceremony."

Walker's brows rose. "A formal Marriage Ritual is a major event."

Barton rocked back and forth on his heels. "Short and simple." He gestured with his chin. "Great party later, at the Temple and Clover Compound."

"I note your request," Walker replied. "As I was saying, if you want a potent Marriage Ritual tonight, you should do the cleansings and meditations to prepare for it. Noonbell hasn't struck, you have time for the traditional preparatory septhours to ensure a powerful Marriage Ritual tonight."

Barton hissed and stepped back. "Cleansings and meditations!" Easy to understand he preferred sex to just the opposite.

Walker held out his arms. "Go take care of the rituals for a groom. Give Enata to me."

"No." He squeezed her so tightly that she squeaked.

T'Willow strolled up and used a FirstFamily command voice. "Give Enata to me."

"No!" Enata heard the snap of Barton's teeth after that word.

≈ Chapter 6 ≈

Barton began backing away toward the doorway and the glider he must have arrived in. That clued her that the man didn't teleport well. He might not be able to teleport the two of them. She could, of course, but didn't think it appropriate to take him to D'Licorice Residence or the PublicLibrary, the places she knew best.

And now her brain began to clear from the effervescence of the potion that had made her so open to everything, she thought she'd prefer to conduct the traditions of a bride on her wedding day. From the compelling link between her and Barton, she'd be married to him for the rest of her life. She supposed she should free herself from him.

Her father stomped up to them. "You give me my daughter *right now.*"

Barton nearly growled, *did* glare at T'Licorice, but after a full minute, transferred Enata to her father's arms. She sighed and went a little limp in the familiar embrace. Papa didn't feel at all like Barton. Her father took her out of her lover's reach and set her down.

Her mother and Barton's mother looked up from where they'd been conversing.

D'Licorice said, "Twinmoons rise is mid-evening bell tonight. A very propitious time for beginning a Marriage Ritual." She flicked a hand at Barton. "Take yourself off and prepare for the ceremony."

Barton huffed. "I need to . . . walk the Family labyrinth, meditate in the grove, *cleanse and purify* myself for the ceremony." His nostrils widened, he marched the two paces to Enata, lifted her hand and kissed the back of it. "I will see you later, beloved. 'Parting is such sweet sorrow.' And it is." He tapped his chest. "Sweet because I met you, held you, and I know I will see you and wed you and love you this evening. But leaving you is difficult."

Walker stiffened, stared at his brother. "You read poetry? You *quote* poetry!"

Barton fisted his hand. "Keep it up, brother, and you'll take part in a marriage ritual with a broken nose."

"He is wonderful," Enata sighed.

Sweeping a graceful, formal bow to her, he kissed her fingers. "Later," he said huskily.

She really enjoyed being in Barton's arms.

Enata's father took her arm and brought it firmly through his, leading her away. Her mother took a package from the Willow housekeeper and came to Enata's other side. Enata looked over her shoulder at Barton. None of the other men stood near him, not even his brother.

"Until later, beloved." He *smoldered* at her. The timbre of his voice matched a hot intention coming from him through their bond. He wanted to make love with her as soon as possible. She swallowed.

An instant later she and her parents had teleported to the small room that housed the iron spiral staircase down to the HouseHeart, the core intelligence of D'Licorice Residence, where the "brain," HouseStones, lived. Her parents excused themselves and Enata ran down the stairs, descending deep under the Residence to begin a meditation session.

The HouseHeart burbled at her for thirty-five minutes, thrilled that all its Family had now been been matched. Totally approving that they'd spent an incredible amount of gilt on the appointment for Enata. And as she regulated her breathing and looked at the individual facets of the quartz ceiling, she understood that when she and Barton had children, whomever needed a matchmaker's appointment would get one. Neither her parents nor her sister and Jace, both HeartMated couples, had required help in determining their mates.

As Enata pondered the situation, she realized that it may have taken her and Barton Clover long years to meet, they were so outside of each other's circles. And by the time they met, they might have changed enough so they weren't an exceptional match.

She'd been blessed, by this Residence and her Family. No, she didn't have a HeartMate, but that could be all to the good. HeartMate marriages were tough on the ones left behind. As soon as she'd understood about HeartMates and her parents and her sister, Enata had realized that. Someday her parents would die within a year of each other. Someday the same would happen to Glyssa and her HeartMate.

Before today, Enata had faced the fact that she could very well be left alone.

Now it was different and a big sigh escaped her.

The HouseHeart, a round room carved from bedrock, the basic personality of the Residence, had fallen silent. Enata stood and went to the fountain in the west, placed her hands under the second bubbling tier, and began the first ritual of her wedding day. "HouseHeart, please say the personal blessing for a Bride of a Daughter of the House for me."

"I will do so," said the HouseHeart in a multi-toned voice that echoed with all the personalities from the past and the Residence's own present voice. "D'Licorice and T'Licorice wait outside to join you to bless you in your next ritual circuit of the HouseHeart." Which meant she'd spent more time meditating than they'd anticipated.

Did they think she doubted this exceptional love match? She did, but not as much as they.

She curled her toes into the thick hybrid grass of Earth and Celta, set her mind in those toes and inhaled, pulling the strength of the planet through her. It tingled like sparkles of light. And she chanted the first prayer of gratitude and blessing.

* * *

Barton strode out of T'Willow Residence into the courtyard where Walker's glider sat, complete with the primary driver-guard Barton had assigned to his brother. After meeting Enata, Barton was surprised he'd been able to string two words together, let alone quote poetry or briefly consider the future of the Family. Now he had two Families to protect. Five new people added to his responsibilities shouldn't upset his balance, but they were *not Clovers.*

And one was *her.* His lover, his soon-to-be-TONIGHT wife. His woman.

Walker caught up with him, grabbed his elbow. "Hold on and I'll 'port you to your house."

Barton grunted.

"What, no poetry?" Walker teased.

With a sneer, Barton looked at his brother. "You should try poetry. It works with women. I've always known that."

Walker's expression smoothed. "I'm very glad you found a good woman to love. Now let's get you home to Clover Compound, the cleansing and other procedures—"

"Dad and a couple of other of the male elders can help me out with the prayers and pre-ritual stuff, but *not Uncle Pink.* He would drive me crazy with his fancy notions."

Stiffening, Walker looked hurt and Barton recalled how he'd spent nearly every minute with his brother on Walker's wedding day. Hell! "I need you to take care of the organizational matters." Barton scrubbed his scalp. "And I must walk our labyrinth by myself. This situation . . ." *Love, so quickly and soon.* "Has knocked me off course."

"Good, since you need to let the matter of Savi and Balansa go. And good that you're doing a walking meditation. I'll join you when you're finished, after I delegate certain matters. If this takes place in GreatCircle Temple, the High Priest and Priestess may officiate. Other great nobles might attend."

"Everything must be as perfect as we can make it," Barton said, in unison with Walker. They all strove to ensure the Family would be well respected.

"Hang on," Walker gripped Barton's right biceps, counted down, then teleported them into the mainspace of Barton's house.

The very dusty mainspace with battered

furniture and graying walls of once-white. Barton winced.

"I'll get a crew in to clean this place up," Walker said. He punched Barton on the shoulder. "Go take a waterfall."

And so the rest of the day began. A day he'd never quite recall, passing in odd lurching moments as he waited through the long septhours for night to claim his woman as wife and lover.

* * *

As Barton strode into the huge main chamber of GreatCircle Temple, he automatically scanned it for threats and noted who showed up for his wedding. A quick jump of his heart showed him that Walker and the Clovers—and probably the Licorices, too — had drawn a good amount of the FirstFamily nobles, those highest of the high, descendants of the people who'd paid for the starships to colonize Celta.

The Hollys were there, but Barton had worked for that Family. Also attending were the nobles of his generation with whom he'd had sparring lessons since he'd been a boy. He considered them all friends. Walker's in-laws, the Grove FirstFamily, another small Family, were there.

A gentle warmth spread through Barton as he walked with measured pace to the altar at the center of the room. There awaited the High Priest and High Priestess of Celta, whom he'd barely met. The Clovers didn't have any up-and-coming people in the priest or priestesshood. He'd have liked Family handling this, as everything else. Barton gulped and inclined his head to the pair. Then he turned south to face one of the four main doors, awaiting his bride.

A terrible buzzing throbbed in his head, kept beat with his heart. What if she had doubts, didn't come? Sliding his eyes to her side of the room, he saw Enata's sister and HeartMate. That slightly reassured him.

His parents stood close, arms twined around each other's waist, his mother holding a softleaf for tears. His two brothers and two sisters, along with their children and Familiar Companions, fronted the rest of many Clovers.

He settled into his balance and tightened his jaw, waiting, then became aware of music. Wonderful wedding ritual music played on flute and harp and strings, so he breathed to it, understanding from the piece that Enata should make her entrance no more than three minutes from now, right on schedule.

The longest three minutes of his life.

Stoically, Barton stood. His gaze snagged on Vinni T'Vine, the prophet, and anxiety surged. Yeah, Vinni was a friend of Barton's, and yeah, four out of five times fighting with Vinni, Barton could take him out. But no one in the whole world wanted the prophet's gaze and Flair focused on them. Then Vinni grinned and winked at him and relief sifted through Barton just as the music changed tempo to the Bride's Entrance.

His gaze shot to the south door and his whole chest squeezed as he saw her. Of course between the liquored up meeting that morning and now, he'd had his own doubts about the strength of his attraction, even though the immediate bond still spun between them.

Her beauty struck him, more than physical, the

whole of her presence as she glided into the room. Her hair waved softly below her shoulders and the lightspells picked up an occasional hint of gold in the red, lighter than it had seemed this morning. All of her seemed lighter, less serious, looser. She wore a gown of deep blue, sewn with crystals—the night and stars. And looked at him with vulnerable hope in her eyes.

He'd never let her down.

* * *

Enata trod hesitantly through the large doors and into the inner chamber of GreatCircle Temple, between her parents. Her hands shook around the bouquet of flowers. People filled the place! More than she'd ever seen at an inside ritual before.

She swallowed and blinked at everyone waiting and watching her, easy to see since several spell globes circled the dome like tiny suns. Most of those attending were Clovers. An incredibly large Family for Celtans. The little voice in her head that collected facts stated that the average nuclear family size of the Clovers included five children. Her stomach clenched, but she lifted her chin, realizing that she wanted children. Five would be fine.

Then her gaze rose from the crowd to look at Barton. The man who'd give her those children, and her mind seemed to fire into mist. Big, tough. Sexy.

As she left the crowd behind and walked through the free space toward the altar, a hum of approval rippled through the crowd. Mostly from the Clover Family, particularly his parents, and his powerfully Flaired brother, Walker. A warmth unfurled inside her as she sensed the love of brother for brother that reflected the love that bound all the Clover Family together.

Soon she'd be part of a large—no, massive—Family, and she cherished the idea of emotional warmth. Her own Family tended to more logic than emotion and didn't often express their affection for each other in public, or even privately. She wanted more close connections.

And then she reached the altar and her parents faded back behind her, as Barton's brother, Walker, and his parents stood behind him. So close to Barton that she could touch him. She wanted to touch him. Absolutely no doubts now. This was right.

As if he sensed her conviction, Barton rocked toward her, caught himself and stopped.

The Priestess and Priest led the opening chant and people naturally arranged themselves into a ritual circle, guests of the bride alternating with guests of the groom when possible. The circle was cast and consecrated.

And magic throbbed in the atmosphere, composed of Flair and well wishes . . . of love. One blessing seemed doubled and tripled and quadrupled in the orb of the sacred space, arching overhead and down below into the planet.

Everything faded for Enata but Barton, his intense blue gaze, the lean lines of his face, his strong posture, the masculine grace of his gestures, the deep tone of his words. She flowed away on chants she didn't really hear, only experienced through him. She thought he felt the same.

Her voice came out steady and loud for the vows, as did his.

Their forearms were tied together with colorful ribbons, an outward manifestation of the inner bond pulsing between them. By that time she'd been so sensitized by the ceremony that his skin sent a frisson along her nerves and began a slow wave of lusty heat cycling through them.

They lit the unity candle, the two other candles lit from that flame passed around the circle to cross and return. They drank first from the loving cup. A great shout came when the cup returned from being ritually sipped by everyone. The Priest and Priest intoned the final blessing, announced them as husband and wife. Then a beautiful lilting melody swept through the room as the ritual ended and her hand was caught by her father, who grinned—grinned!—at her, loosened her ribbon bonds with Barton to a good two meters, and the dancing began.

After the first dance the drinking started, too, with lots of toasts. She even lifted a mug to her Family, letting tears trickle down her face as she spoke of her love for them, including her sister's new HeartMate. Enata could feel Jace in their Family bond—brash and impulsive—as her parents and sister no doubt felt Barton—durable and reliable.

Every other heartbeat brought a wash of Clover threads to her, ready to be bound with her, overwhelming if she let them.

One of the large circle dances stopped and her father dropped her hand. Barton swung her out into the middle of the huge floor, holding her close and moving her faster than the beat of the music.

"Barton!"

He grinned. "Don't fit your notion of proper,

huh? But you kept right up with me."

She narrowed her eyes at his deliberate bad grammar. "Barton."

He whisked her into another tight turn. "You're keeping up with me, and that isn't easy, for a fighter or a dancer." He beamed, lowered her into a deep dip. She slapped his shoulder, completely dependent on him for her balance, and completely trusting him.

"What you want to lead?" A short laugh and this time his brows stayed up. "That isn't—ain't—going to happen."

"Oh?"

"Nope." He straightened, so forcefully that he drew her off of her feet.

"You think because you are superior in strength and can toss me around like a doll—"

He did! He actually threw her in the air and caught her! Then let her slide against his body. His very aroused body.

She opened her mouth, couldn't think of a word to say and shut it.

Looking smug, he said, "So much for your scolding. Ah, I know you already, my lady. A sweet and tart lady." He nuzzled her neck and to her appalled surprise, licked her under her ear!

"Your tartness is obvious, but your sweetness only evident at close quarters." He danced her out of the crowd and to the wall, pressed her against it, stroked her jaw. When she parted her lips, his eyes fired. He let his body lean against hers and for the first time in her life she craved sex.

≈ Chapter 7 ≈

"Let's get out of here," Barton said.

"How?" Enata asked.

"Teleportation."

She didn't think he could teleport and she didn't know the light or the space where they'd need to land at Clover Compound.

"You do want to go to—"

"Our house in Clover Compound. Yeah."

Their house. A house she'd never seen. She'd never seen Clover Compound either.

Barton waved an arm at a curvy woman with dark brown hair and a cheerful manner. Enata recognized her as the musician and composer, Trif Clover Winterberry.

With a wink at them, and a wave to a man and children, she crossed to them, beamed. "Greetyou again, Enata Licorice *Clover*."

Effervescent with happiness, freer than she'd been for a long time, Enata let laughter pour from her, tipping her head back. Barton's face filled her vision, and his lips locked onto hers. His arms caged her close, against his erect masculinity, and she pressed against him, took his tongue into her mouth.

Vaguely, she felt a woman's arm around her back, knew that as her own and Barton's minds hazed, Trif's stayed crystal clear . . . and amused.

If the woman counted down for the teleportation, Enata didn't know. Only a sudden whoosh, and she pulled her tongue behind her own teeth reflexively. But they landed as gently as a flower petal drifting to the ground.

"Enjoy yourselves," Trif said. "I'm going back to the party!" She vanished.

Soft, mellow light and the gentle fragrance of summer flowers wafted to Enata. She drew away a step from Barton.

He stiffened as she glanced around, said gruffly, "Haven't been paying attention to my space." He shrugged. "It's a starter house for a couple and suited my needs."

Not at all homey or comfortable like her rooms in D'Licorice Residence. She considered. "This doesn't reflect what I know of the quality and attractiveness of Clover Fine Furnishings."

Before he could draw breath, she leaned against him. "And is completely uninteresting at the moment when compared to the very fine and attractive Clover man I have." She hesitated. "My husband."

He expelled a harsh breath, stared at her. Emotion flickered in his eyes—a hint of fear? Surely not. When he spoke, his voice had roughened. He took her hands, gazed down at her.

Come, Madam, come, all rest my powers defy,
Until I labor, I in labor lie.
The foe oft-times having the foe in sight,
Is tir'd with standing though he never fight.

She shivered as the poetry in that powerful voice caressed her, then answered the innuendos with her own truth. "It has been a long day of . . . yearning for you."

A laugh and he swept her into his arms, pivoted and strode to the staircase, sprinted up them and down the hallway to a bedroom, again minimally furnished. One bedsponge big enough for the two of them. A new no-time food storage unit. Two spell globes in pale yellow circled the room, casting warm light.

Touching her shoulder tabs he said, "Wedding robe *off!*" The bespelled cloth dropped from her and she stepped from the pool of it, then it whisked away to hang in the open closet.

She didn't, quite, grit her teeth. Now she stood only in breastband over her very modest bust and wispy pantlettes.

Gently he curved his right hand over her left shoulder and she felt the hardness of calluses that he had developed. Heat flooded her.

Your gown going off, such beautious state reveals,
As when from flow'ry meads th'hills shadow steals

This time his voice trembled and giddiness surged. He liked the way she looked! He placed both palms over her breasts and her nipples puckered at the thought of those fingers stroking her bare breasts. Petting her lower where she was going wet.

He continued skipping and mixing lines and verses. That he should know the sexy poem in the first place, and should recall it now when her own mind fogged with desire, impressed her. Especially that he could improvise and match it with their loving. Then he knelt at her feet and she swayed, put her own hands on his shoulders to steady herself. He flinched, and though his head bowed, she thought she heard a low groan.

One large hand ringed her ankle, lifted her foot shod in special wedding slippers, white with crystals on the top, soft leather below, but good for dancing. She didn't want to dance. She wanted to have sex—to *make love*. Her whole body throbbed with need.

He slipped her shoe off, drew his fingers along her sole and her foot curled and her fingers dug into his thick shoulder muscles. He didn't seem to notice. Because he was looking straight at her thin, lacy pantlettes. His nostrils widened. Could he *smell* her arousal?

Embarrassed heat washed through her, flushing her skin from forehead down her torso. He rumbled a hum of satisfaction, licked his lips, cleared his throat and said, as he reached for her other foot:

Now off with those shoes, and then softly tread
In this, love's hallow'd temple, this soft bed.

He stripped that shoe, tossed it aside, rose, and set his hands on her waist, lifted her again until he stood, holding her off her feet. His eyes appeared wild. "Trying," he gritted out. "Trying to be romantic, to slow down so I don't take you hard and fast . . . 'soft bed.'" He looked at the bedsponge and his arms flexed as if he'd throw her on that soft mattress. "Wait, gotta kiss you."

Not in the poem, but she liked the notion. He brought her close and she wrapped her legs around him, angled her hips so her throbbing point of need could be against his hard body. They both shuddered, then his mouth met hers and she felt the plush of his lips against her own passion swollen ones.

Mouth to mouth, then their lips opened and they were breath to breath, and tongue to tongue. The flavor of him exploded through her, just *right*. Perfect. She stopped rubbing her tongue against his, dueling with him so intimately, to suck in his lower lip and nibble.

Another groan ripped from him, she felt the vibration of it in her mouth. She moved against him, teasing her breasts and her sex to heightened sensuality those points of her own. Her bare arms brushed against his slightly perspiring chest and shoulders.

"No!" he snapped. "I *will* do this right." He pulled her limbs away from him, placed her on her feet. Her mind spun and her knees wobbled.

She couldn't focus until his ruddy face, wide eyes, entered her vision. His mouth lifted at the corner and eyes narrowed. "Now for the very best of that damn poem." He took her wrists, pushed them behind her and manacled them in one strong hand. That steadied her balance but she found herself arching toward him.

A smile edged his lips. Gently, he squeezed her left nipple with the fingers of his other hand. Whimpers of need escaped her lips . . . His hand moved to the tip of her other breast, plucked it, and she felt her cheeks heat with the delight of lust flowing through her body.

The hand that held her wrists touched the curve of her derriere. He cleared his throat, and when phrases came again they sounded raw and ragged:

> *License my roving hands, and let them go,*
> *Behind, before, above, between, below.*

And he touched her like that, little strokes that caused tension to spiral up, tighten inside her. With "behind," his free hand curved over her bottom, barely traced the cleft.

"Before." He grazed his hand over her breasts until her nipples poked heavily against the fabric of her breastband.

"Above." The pad of his thumb swept along her mouth, her darting tongue quick enough to lick it and she tasted salt.

"Between." Yes, his voice deepened on that word, and his fingers slid under the waistband of her pantlettes and down to the very top of her sex, stopped with no more than a fingertip parting her. Yes, between. He must have felt her dampness.

"Below." A hoarse whisper. His face had flushed. His features seemed more blunt. More masculine. More of a man, a lover, ready to take his woman and she ached to be taken. His large finger glided downward, feathering the nub of sensation and she trembled, then he continued onward to the opening of her body. Yes.

Yes, yes, yes, yes, yes!

He withdrew from her, his hands from her body, took a pace back. Stared at her as she trembled before him and the poem rushed from him and she could barely hear the cadence of it, understand the lines:

O my . . . new-found-land,
My kingdom, safeliest when with one man man'd,
My mine of precious stones: my emperie,
How blest am I in this discovering thee!

His tone changed slightly as he said, "How blessed I am in discovering you today." He touched one of the remaining ribbons that had bound them together, a licorice red, that was wrapped around his wrist gave her the next line:

To enter in these bonds, is to be free;

She nodded. When he remained too far away from her, out of reach, she touched the green ribbon on her left wrist, one prettily engraved in gold with a large Celtic knot in the shape of a four leaf Clover. And she repeated that line back to him: "*To enter in these bonds, is to be free.*" Certainly her heart soared, and her spirit expanded. She felt freer than ever before. With him.

He grinned, his expression so full of happiness, and at wedding *her* that her chest constricted in awe. One long pace forward and his smile changed to pure masculine intensity. A brawny arm settled like a bar behind her back and once more his hand went under her pantlettes, this time between her thighs until the length and width of it covered her sex.

"'*Then where my hand is set, my seal shall be,*" he murmured.

Full passion pounded within her and she closed her eyes. Her entire body had become one sensitive organ. She hungered for him to thrust inside her, seal them together. A long minute passed with her enjoying the embrace before she realized he waited for something from her. So she said aloud the only words that floated to her mind. "Yes, husband. Yes, Barton. Yes, let's make love."

"I will do this right." It sounded like a vow. She noticed sweat at his temples.

"You are doing this right. Everything you've done today has been right," she whispered.

He closed his eyes, and his face tightened. Slowly he removed his hand from between her legs and she made a lost sound as he withdrew.

> "'*Full nakedness! All joys are due to thee,*
> *As souls unbodied, bodies uncloth'd must be,*
> *To taste whole joyes.*
> *To teach thee I am naked first,'*" he panted.

Then he dipped his head. "To show you I am as vulnerable as you, my dearest Enata." A Word had his clothes falling from him and he stood, nude. Clothes hid the true beauty of the man, his contoured muscles, well outlined with the sheen of perspiration.

Of course her stare went to his erection. Magnificent. Her breath came so fast her mind went dizzy, then she tensed her jaw. He had given her exquisite foreplay. She could only do the same. With a wave of fingers she sent her bespelled breastband and pantlettes to the cleanser, then lifted her arms to wrap them around his neck. His pupils widened as her flushed and plumped breasts lifted, her nipples tight. She shivered as she stepped closer, his erection pressing into her abdomen, hot, thick, ready.

Her own sex pulsed, ready for him. She leaned close and kissed his chin, licked the faint stubble of his beard, marshaled the last line of the poem so she could modify it, say it, then let her body rule. "Why, then . . ." She stopped, her voice must be stronger, full of the passion and the desire and the knowledge that this man was her man and she claimed him as he claimed her:

"'*Why, then,*
What needest I to have more covering than a man?'"

He groaned. This time he did pick her up and toss her onto the bedsponge and followed her down. His body came over hers, she opened her legs wide, wide so he found his place between them and thrust heavily into her, the feel of him filling her, fulfilling her, freeing her.

≈ Chapter 8 ≈

Barton felt Enata clench around him in her orgasm. He gritted his teeth and tried to hold back his own completion, skate on the edge of fabulous pleasure and exquisite need. She gasped, angled her hips, grabbed him around the shoulders, and he was lost.

He'd been semi-erect the whole damn day and he couldn't practice one more instant of patience. He let fierce need blast away his control. He thrust into her once, twice, and climaxed.

Just before he collapsed on his slender new wife, he rolled them to their sides . . . on a too damn small bedsponge. He needed a bigger bed. No, *they* needed a bigger bed, bedroom, house.

A small sigh escaped her, and he studied her, her fine-boned face, the pale, near translucent skin so delicate he could see pale blue veins in her temple. She seemed to consider her body as a housing for her mind.

His body was his best tool, cared for and honed as a matter of security . . . and, yes, pride.

Her eyes had closed and he sensed her drifting to sleep as the busyness of her mind faded into occasional thoughts. She, too, must have been tried by the unexpected events of the day. He frowned, lifted a finger to trace her high cheekbone. She appeared strung too tightly, was too thin, and her mind held a heaviness of coping with recent trauma. What?

He knew too little about her and her of him, but instinctively he drew her into his arms, against him so he could protect her.

She snuggled and gave that last exhale before sleep.

His whole body loosened, and not just because of the most incredible sex he'd ever had.

He'd done it! He'd claimed his woman *right*.

When he'd been left alone with her, with no extraordinary events carrying them along, he'd realized that he must cement their bond. It had started as a tendril spinning between them due to potions and initial attraction. He had to make it solid and real.

Enata's father's earlier derisive comments, barely noticed at the time, had worked on Barton. The Clovers, though a rising Family, were recently ennobled. Only Walker, Barton's half-brother resulting from a fling with a highly Flaired noblewoman, had enough psi power to raise them up, though the younger generations would be more powerful. Especially those of the Clovers who married into other Families with potent Flair. Like Walker. Like their cuz Trif.

Like Barton himself. During the long preparations of that day, he'd been informed that the Licorice Family, and, more importantly, the PublicLibrary the Licorices tended, had been founded within the first half-decade of the colonists' landing. Over four hundred and fifteen years before.

Barton couldn't match his new lady in Flair. He didn't even have enough power to teleport. She was at the top of her profession.

As he was with his own, but that was due to physical skill and dedicated training.

Yeah, he'd felt that strand stretching between them had been too fragile, since they came from two very different worlds. And he'd wanted her from the moment he'd seen her. *Did* love her from that instant, knew in his gut and the marrow of his bones that she was the right woman for him.

He'd seen her eyes widen, felt pleasure spurt through that tiny bond when he'd quoted poetry, so he damn well kept it up. Would keep it up. A few lines had worked on women before, but the effect on Enata—her heart and spirit opening to him—had been significant. At least in that particular he knew what she liked and he'd make sure he'd give it to her, along with loving.

She needed love, to be surrounded by love. Pretty obvious her Family prized the cool and logical and didn't go in for displays of affection. *His* Family would help with that. As sleep tempted, he fumbled for his mind link with Walker, shot his brother a thought, *My wife needs loving Family.*

We got that, Walker replied. *My HeartM—, my wife knows Enata. We'll be hands on with Enata.*

Good, Walker sent back sleepily, smiled. Yeah, his Family was good. Walker had stopped from saying "HeartMate," since Barton had no HeartMate.

He gathered his wonderful, beautiful, amazing wife closer still. And her hand dropped to his sex.

She knew what he liked, and he was sure she'd give it to him.

* * *

A septhour before dawn they woke, starving. They'd made love several times in the night, more than Enata had ever done, advantages to having a very physical man, though she understood it would be necessary for her to become more physical herself. She definitely needed more stamina and, judging by the way he'd tossed her around earlier, some more mass, too. And muscles.

She'd never have the muscles he did, but she should be able to hold her own more than she had, though she could, of course, counter his muscles with the strength of her Flair.

Their last bout had taken place in the waterfall, one smaller than she thought this master suite should have. She grinned and put a sashay into her short walk to the no-time, hoping Barton couldn't hear her stomach grumbling.

He groaned and she heard the flop of him as he fell from sitting to the bedsponge. "Don't tempt me, woman! I need food before we celebrate our marriage again!"

Stopping at the low no-time, she glanced over her shoulder, found him staring avidly at her and appearing more interested in another round of sex than his words indicated. "Is it a celebration, this marriage?" She sounded more doubtful than she wanted.

"Absolutely, yes," he answered immediately. He sat back up with impressive ease.

"Good," she said, examining the contents of the no-time for food easy to eat naked, nothing too hot, cold or needing a lot of utensils. She settled on a large fruit and cheese platter and bent down to take out the plate.

Barton moaned again. "Foood . . . maybe. Maybe sex—"

"Food," she stated, throwing a cover over him and sitting next to him, ready to share a meal. Neither of them had touched the large wedding banquet. They'd danced instead. "What sounds best, fruit or cheese?"

"Fruit," he said. She popped a dark grape into his mouth.

"The selection of cheeses is wonderful!" she said. Before she spoke the last word, he plunked a cube of nutty-flavored cheese in her mouth. She swiped his finger with her tongue, pleased when he shuddered.

"I'm glad," she said, actually speaking before she thought, just letting a feeling out.

"About what?" he mumbled around a slice of fruit. He swallowed. "Specifically."

She found herself grinning. "Right now that we're eating a meal together."

He grunted. "Another good activity for couples." He put his hand under her chin and nudged her to kiss him. "I have sweetness on my mouth and want a taste of my tart lady."

Leaning toward him she slid the tip of her tongue between his lips. "And I want to taste my sweet, sweet man."

He scowled at her, but she trailed her tongue across his mouth and the juice from fruit mixed with the savory of the cheeses she'd sampled, exploding in flavor. With a gasp, she pulled back, realized she'd closed her eyes and couldn't see his face, and raised her lashes. She caught a look of tenderness that made her ache with happiness. Refusing to censor herself, she said, "With you I experience the true richness of every sensation."

He jerked back, took her hands in his own, ignoring her sticky fingers. "I am glad." He opened his mouth as if to say something, closed it and looked out the window, a lighter gray rectangle against the wall, then back at her. "It's been a magical day and night. I don't want it to end." A slow smile curved his lips. "They'll let us stay here, in my house—our house—in our bed all day." He jiggled his eyebrows in question.

Oh, yes, she wished for more sensational moments. Giddy irresponsibility flowed through her, along with the equally devil-may-care feeling shooting along their bond from Barton, accompanied by a look that touched her heart.

"Let's!" she agreed.

"All right, we'll continue this celebration. Is there any chilled fizz-wine in there?" He nodded to the no-time.

"I don't know, but I saw a very expensive vintage of springreen wine. Your brother and Family value you, to give that to you for your own personal use."

"Ah." He picked up a wedge of dark yellow cheese and munched, staring at her. "My brother's very happy with recent events." One side of his mouth lifted in an ironic smile.

She scanned his body, head to toe, and sent him a sultry look. She knew how important this after-sex . . . after *loving* time was, but the man stirred her. "Because you dated so many women?" She could see that, a handsome, very virile man like him.

He laughed shortly. "No. Just the opposite." Now he grimaced. "Maybe I did when younger. Lately I've cared for nothing except my work."

Shaking his head, he continued, "Recently I've been determined to track down a couple of cuzes." His mouth flattened. "We failed them and they left, are lost."

That twanged some sorrowful chord inside her and she frowned, trying to pinpoint why.

And while she focused inwardly, he pounced.

She let him roll her to her back, then, with a Word, removed the food and platter from the bed to a nightstand. Then she used Flair to toss himself and her back over so she straddled him, enjoying his startled expression. As she kissed his cheek, she decided that she wanted to taste several particular parts of him, returning the favor of his delightful exploration in the night.

Her body flushed at the thought.

A quick tussle later, a fabulous out-of-time sensual experience like no other, and he'd collapsed into sleep beside her. She lay awake, surprise at herself holding off sleep.

She'd have liked to have blamed the wild sex and the tenderness and the intense, intimate connection on the potion they'd taken the previous day. But she raised to her elbow and studied him, this incredible man who'd exhausted her, and whom she'd exhausted—and all she could feel was that basic, instinctive attraction. *Mate.* Perhaps not a HeartMate, but more elemental, like she recognized him in the cells of her body, the marrow of her bones.

Such a gorgeous man, as if he'd been plucked from her mind and her ideal embodied: tall, large, muscular, not at all a scholarly build. Dark hair and deep blue eyes that made her shiver with desire. A face more rugged than handsome, showing character. So much sexier than Glyssa's man—stop that thought, no comparisons. To compare the men was beneath Enata. And no more judgments. She'd have to work on that. But there was no sexier man in the world than Barton Clover.

She'd won this man, or he'd won her.

* * *

Enata slept fitfully. The man in her bed, radiating heat, snoring softly, was luscious. The bedsponge was too soft. And the window seemed to be in the wrong direction. For a few minutes she listened to the quiet of the house, of the courtyards of the Clover Compound beyond. Nothing stirred, and if she was lonely she couldn't raise her voice and speak to an intelligent Residence. Not that she'd done that often, but the possibility had gotten her through some dark winter nights.

As if the loneliness had pulsed from her to him, Barton awoke and reached for her and this time the loving proceeded slowly, with an intimacy the dark engendered, with exchanged tender, lingering touches that pleased them both. Quietly, wordlessly, they joined and rocked to completion.

The next time she woke, Barton had left the bed and she was alone, though she heard the sound of a nearby flowing waterfall.

Slipping from the bed, she donned a light silkeen robe of pale green.

She didn't know if she liked the idea of only living with one person, no matter how beloved. Yet he'd moved from his family home to be alone in this narrow house. That demonstrated a disparate mind-set between them. Then, as the door slammed open and no fewer than ten women flowed in, she reconsidered.

≈ Chapter 9 ≈

"Welcome to the Clover Family, to the circle of Clover women," trilled a pregnant woman younger than Enata. She didn't recall meeting the cheerful girl who gave her a hearty hug. "I'm Xanthia Clover, the last one marrying into the Family before you."

"Welcome!" the others chorused, gathering around her. One smoothed the robe over her shoulders, another patted her head and she felt her curly disarrayed hair fall into place. "We're so glad to have you as part of the Family," someone else said.

"Let's give you a lovely breakfast!" said an older woman.

"I—" Enata started. What happened to staying in bed all day? "Barton?"

"We told him telepathically that breakfast is ready. He'll join us as soon as he's done with a waterfall."

"The no-time—"

The older woman snorted. "It doesn't have special wedding morning omelettes." She gave a decided nod. "Made to order, whatever you like in it. The food storage unit doesn't contain enough porcine strips for you and Barton. That man can eat. And he needs to keep his strength up."

Rollicking laughter and a nudge of an elbow. Along with the noise of the women and the grumbling of her stomach came the sense of new connections with these women. Enough to daze her.

The Clover Family connections grew every second she spent with Barton's relatives, began to thread through her, spurred by the ritual the night before and the vows Enata had made.

They swept her in a tide of femininity down the stairs of Barton's house, she only kept from falling by the press of bodies, then outside—in only her robe! More eyes, women and men, stared at her from the large rectangular courtyard, and from people at windows facing the yard. Just having their stares focused on her seemed to stimulate more links.

She gasped for breath.

"Come along, Enata," said a woman who Enata thought was the head female elder. Though she'd been introduced last night, Enata didn't recall her name. Barton's bond with that woman showed huge and thick and surged to hit Enata. She swayed.

Where was Barton? She sensed he still soaped in the waterfall. Another irritation that she stood here in the courtyard in her robe, no matter how warm the summer morning, and he didn't stand with her. Toes curling into a crack in the flagstones, she stopped to look back at his house, saw nothing but a brown brick building with no remarkable features.

Two women took her arms, helping her to walk to the horizontal wing at the end of the courtyard, though she didn't know that she cared to go with them anymore.

She saw Walker Clover's HeartMate, Sedwy Grove Clover, near the other end of the courtyard. Enata knew Sedwy, had helped the woman with her research and career in anthropology. "Sedwy!" she called, but other voices drowned out her cry, people exiting their houses to shout greetings to Enata, comment on the wedding the night before.

Barton, please request your ladies don't crowd me.

She felt his laugh through her bond. *Just tell them to back off.*

All right. "Stop this!" she shouted. "Give me a little room, please!"

They didn't seem to hear her, kept conversations going among themselves, talking around her, exclaiming at the bonds they began to feel to her, and through her to the Licorice Family.

She muttered a mind-clearing spell. It would deplete her Flair, but she wanted coherent thought. *Barton, please call off your ladies.* She kept her mental voice crisp. *Before I do something to alienate them.* As they had alienated her? Was this some kind of test? Perhaps.

She *could* become an integral member of this large Family.

With that conclusion, the stirring threads of the Clovers' links to her through Barton tugged at Enata's insides, a nauseating wave. Yes, she was bonding with all the Clovers. They milled around her. As they moved it seemed those threads turned into a shroud, wrapping around her, binding her arms, crossing over her mouth so she couldn't speak.

So she sent a mental call, *Barton, can you come*?

In a minute, babe, he replied, a little absently. She blinked. Obviously she was no longer his sole focus, perhaps not his primary one. She understood that, but it hurt.

Panting, she held out for a minute, two, as people propelled her into a large kitchen area that held two long tables. Her mind did slow swoops and her balance tilted. Two women yet framed her.

Why were they doing this?

She thought she sent the pointed question to them, along with her discomfort, and a tidal wave of affection struck her.

Too much! Too many people and minds and emotions!

Doubling over, she concentrated on the plank flooring to steady herself, then glanced up. People were talking to her, their mouths moving, loud buzzing in her ears.

Somewhere, in the back of her mind, in the back of her skull, throbbed a *need* to return to the PublicLibrary vaults. To the coolness and the quiet, the emptiness with no press of bodies.

She was so *tired* of feeling ill. It seemed like she'd struggled with sickness the whole month.

Barton? This time she could barely hear her own thought. Could he?

No answer. No, she couldn't stay.

"Let me go, please," she shrieked, and silence fell over the room filled with Clovers of all ages.

She tottered.

Then she did the desperate and cowardly thing and teleported away to the place she knew best, her bedroom.

Bright sunlight painted a large yellow square on her spread. The scent of the frankincense candles she'd lit for blessings the day before wafted to her nose.

"Residence?" Her voice sounded weak and thin.

"I am here, Enata," it soothed in a male voice. Not Barton's. The Residence waited and quiet wrapped around her.

"Hungry," she muttered. She hadn't eaten much the day before, nothing in the night, a little cheese in the dawn. And she'd participated in a major ritual, danced, made enthusiastic love, barely slept.

She'd failed the Clovers' test, and she didn't care. She didn't know when she could force herself to return to the Compound, all those busy minds and emotions, that still impinged on her. She crumpled.

* * *

Enata was gone!

Barton jerked his attention away from his guards' scry report and the futile inquiry about Savi and Balansa. Walked away from the scry panel.

She'd left him. After one night of extraordinary passion, the minute he stepped away from her, she'd abandoned him. Misery.

Total shock.

As he ran downstairs he shouted to her telepathically. *Enata*!

No answer. Scowling, he listened hard, opened the bond between them—that had narrowed on her side—and found only deep dreams with a dark tinge.

I love you, he sent, and he thought the tension in her dreams eased.

But he didn't know what to do. Whether to go after her or not.

Whether the intelligent Residence would even let him past the threshold. He had too much pride to scry her parents at the PublicLibrary, and her leaving him hurt, dammit.

He stormed into the courtyard, trusting his clothes to soak up the remaining damp from the waterfall, through the too-many-people-hanging-around-for-a-regular-workday and to the kitchen where high babble came from. The cluster of women, including Pink's wife who ran the compound, Aunt Pratty, didn't meet his eyes. Forget the clothes helping rid him of the wet, it could steam off him. The fact that he'd dismissed Enata's concerns just made him angrier—at himself.

"Weren't you all supposed to be loving and supportive?" As was he. He'd noted a darkness of trauma in her, and forgotten about it. He sucked in a deep breath, saw the women had lined up in a semicircle before him.

"All we wanted to do was, uh, feed her breakfast and, uh, maybe figure out what kind of woman she was." But Pratty continued to avoid eye contact. "We didn't have any time to learn her, like we have others."

He loosened his jaw so his teeth didn't clamp together, sank a few centimeters into his balance.

"She seemed snooty," one of his cuzes said.

"What? From the wedding where you saw her? Who else said so? Sedwy knows her, Trif knows of her. Did you ask them?"

"They are busy."

His voice chilled. "You thought it so important that I wed that you near nagged me senseless, chivvied me into an appointment with the best matchmaker of Celta, then you don't accept his recommendation? Don't give *my wife* the respect she deserves?"

Shuffling began. Those closest to the doors faded away.

"We did try to help. We brought her here for

good food. And we all sent her lots of good feelings! Especially when she asked."

He stared at the remaining people in the room. At least twenty-three. More filled the courtyard. "You saw her Family last night. She has both parents, a sister, and a sister's HeartMate. Five people."

"I guess we overwhelmed her," one of his guards taking the afternoon shift mumbled.

"I guess we did," Barton said. He couldn't stand still, couldn't stay in this room that had once been comforting, with what should be equally comforting smells of cooking food.

He'd been abandoned. Rejected by his bride the morning after his wedding. No, he wouldn't go to her. She would have to come to him.

Raising his voice and spearing it into the minds of all his guards, he shouted: *All guards currently off duty, report for sparring practice in the training room.* Mental groans came his way, but he didn't care, he needed to *act.*

Barton spent a good septhour and a half sparring with his men, working off his frustration. Each bout he wondered whether Enata would come back. He sensed when she rose, ate, took a waterfall. And when she cracked the link between them open wider, he couldn't stop the anger and hurt from surging to her, just as he knocked a sloppy guard down. That shocked *Enata*. Good.

Yeah, maybe in the upset of the moment when she'd left, he thought about going after her. Now his pride had risen. No way.

He moved on to train with two more guards.

* * *

Enata awoke much later, weak with hunger and slightly sick. Even before she sat up, she opened her link with Barton, winced at the hard anger coming from him, felt actual physical violence, before he snapped that connection shut.

She swallowed. She had her parents—until they died, and then they'd pass on to the Wheel of Stars within a year of each other, as HeartMates did. But her sister Glyssa would be spending most of her life on the Eastern frontier at the excavation of *Lugh's Spear*. Someday Enata would be alone . . . if she didn't mend the rift with her husband.

Husband. A wonderful word, and Barton was a wonderful man, but they would both need to establish boundaries with each other and their Families, individually and as a unit. Create a Family themselves.

Enata believed that in a true marriage, each partner put the other first, before anyone else. Certainly her parents did that, and Enata had already noted the change in Glyssa since she'd returned from the excavation. Jace was now her most important person after herself. Enata didn't know how to do that yet, with Barton.

* * *

It took Walker Clover negotiating with T'Licorice and pressure from both Families on Enata and Barton for them to meet that afternoon at a neutral location—Landing Park outside the starship *Nuada's Sword*.

She mounted the steps of the white pavilion, then set all openings to privacy shields, made an invisible door in the front that would stop anyone except Barton.

When she felt him arrive at the par, she opened her bond fully. Her stomach tightened with anxiety but a warmth bloomed at the idea of being with him again.

Seeing him stride swiftly across the lawn made her heart nearly beat out of her chest. Before she could discern his features, she identified him by the way he moved, efficiently and with vitality. He leapt up the three wide steps to the pavilion, landing inside with hardly a thump of his large body.

Her arms flung out naturally, leaving the core of her body vulnerable. "I apologize for leaving."

"Leaving *me*." He slapped his chest and his mouth thinned.

She swallowed. "Leaving you."

"Don't do it again. If you need me, yell." One pace brought him to her. He caught her hands, kept them spread and took another step until his solid body brushed hers. "Look at me."

She angled her head up, met his dark blue gaze.

"I will be here for you, always." His voice matched his stare, dead serious. "I don't ever abandon my people."

That resonated through them both, a plucked chord with meaning in the deep dark of her and some vibration she'd understand soon inside him.

"And you will listen to me when I call," she stated.

He nodded. "I screwed up, too," he admitted.

≈ Chapter 10 ≈

His fingers unlinked from hers and he ran his hands from her wrists to her shoulders, and he set them there. "Walker told me you were having problems with all the bonds of our Family."

"Yes, he helped me mute and slow the connections."

"Walker, as the head of the household, and I, as Chief of Security, have stronger links with the other members of our Family than most." Barton cleared his throat. "Previously, when we met and during the wedding ritual, I, uh, sensed you, uh, wanted Family."

"I do!"

"So I told the others, but none of us anticipated what happened."

"I understand. I told that to Walker earlier when he came to talk to me and my father."

Barton inched a little closer, his body pressing into hers. His body was ready for sex. She responded to that knowledge with knee weakening of her own, desire blossoming. His eyes narrowed and a gleam of satisfaction came into his gaze. When he spoke again, his voice was low and rough. "So we were both at fault. But we are wed now, with vows between us."

Vows! She hadn't thought of those when overwhelmed and weary, but she had given promises to Barton and a Licorice did not break promises. Lifting her chin, she said, "I'll say I'm sorry again that I left and hurt you."

"I'll say I'm sorry again that I didn't listen and support you. So. There." He smiled. "If we admit our mutual faults when we argue, it will go much better for us."

She slanted him a look and said precisely, "That is supposing that each of us will be at fault in our arguments, which is not necessarily true."

"There's that tartness I cherish." He grinned.

Since his grin riled her a little she put her fingers on his lips. Immediately he swept his tongue across them and she shivered with sensuality, her sex heating. More, her emotional center, so echoing and frigid this morning after she'd left him—filled and warmed.

He kissed her fingers, brushing them with his full lips. She set aside luscious sensation to think. "We were both to blame. And your Clover ladies—"

"*Our* Clover ladies."

She accepted the correction and rephrased. "Our Clover ladies shouldn't be blamed too much, either. Everything happened so quickly yesterday, such large changes in our lives . . . we reacted instead of taking charge."

He pulled her against his aroused body, but kept his gaze on hers. The beauty of his blue eyes squeezed something inside her. She'd never be indifferent to this man.

Keeping their glances locked, he said, "I wanted to do preparatory rituals, be ready for the ceremony and to be your husband. I wanted you to have a beautiful wedding. That meant letting the Clover wom—ladies organize it. I left the entire situation in their hands, so they might have decided they could intrude in our life. I'll do better."

She framed his face with her hands, liking the

slight prickle of his beard. "I must do better, too." Drawing in a breath, she let it out with soft words. "We'll do better."

He bent his head and brushed her lips with his, a teasing reminder of the pleasure they'd share, that she hoped they'd share all of their lives. She prayed that the love that spun between them would deepen the passion of sex and every day their love would grow.

Just as she sank against him, he drew back, drilled his gaze into hers and said,:

"'Escape me?
Never—
Beloved!
While I am I, and you are you,

So long as the world contains us both,
Me the loving and you the loth
While the one eludes, must the other pursue."'

She shivered at the emotion in his voice, murmured, "I'm not so very loath."

Barton put a hand on her derriere, his eyes fired. "Let's celebrate the ending of our first fight. Teleport us away!"

She wrapped her arms around his waist. "Hold on."

"Never letting go."

She teleported them to the pad near the front of D'Licorice Residence since she didn't know if anyone was inside. If one of her relatives was there, he or she might want to talk, and she didn't.

Barton released his wife slowly. He supposed

they couldn't make love here in the front yard of D'Licorice Residence. The grove of trees, even in summer, didn't look thick enough to hide their activities. Though, by the Lord and Lady, he'd been semi-erect from the moment Walker had confirmed that Enata had agreed to meeting Barton.

Since his pride had taken some beating today, he figured hers had too. Talk about that later, now all he wanted to do was take his wife to bed.

"Where's the nearest bedsponge?" he demanded roughly. Her neck was right there, so he began to lick and nibble on it. She shivered in his arms and he felt the feedback from their link that told him, she, too, rapidly was becoming aroused.

Damn good.

"I take it that you believe we teleported well together."

"Didn't even feel the least bump of landing," he admitted. "But I don't have the Flair to 'port by myself. It was all you."

She shook her head. "No. You added main strength of Flair to our teleportation."

He grunted. "If you say so. Where's the nearest bedsponge?"

Laughing low in her throat, which only hardened him more, she separated so they only held hands and turned toward the graveled gliderway to the front of the Residence, a modest three-storied brick building with white shutters.

She began walking quickly and he kept to her pace though he wanted to scoop her up and run into the house and . . . to wherever her quarters were.

He paused at the door of the Residence. It was

an intelligent Residence. He'd have to keep that in mind and not let his surging passion loose until they'd reached her rooms.

The polished wooden door opened smoothly and silently. A pace beyond the threshold the door closed and Enata stopped, tilting her head, then she told him mentally, *No one of my Family is here.*

He nodded. The weight of the age of the Licorice Family enveloped him.

"Will you introduce me to the oldest and wisest member of your Family?" he asked, spying the scrystone high in the wall that might give the intelligent house eyes.

"Certainly," Enata said. "D'Licorice Residence, this is my husband, Barton Clover."

"I am very pleased to meet you, GentleSir Clover," said the resonant tones of a male persona. "I am most particularly interested in you since it is my understanding that your children with Enata will be my Family."

Enata caught her breath, remarked, "One of Glyssa's and Jace's children could live here."

The Residence replied, "But you will be here in Druida City, dear Enata, and the younger Licorice-Bayrum Family will have their primary home in the east. May I congratulate you, GrandSir Clover, on your taste."

"Thank you."

"You can congratulate me on my taste, too," Enata said, linking arms with him as they took the staircase up, wider than that in his home, but still barely able to accommodate him and his wife. When he—they—chose another house in Clover Compound it would definitely have a staircase he could carry his wife up easily without worrying about bumping her head on the rungs or rail.

They reached the second floor, and turned right to the first door. "My rooms." She set his hand on the door latch and he felt a tingle. "My door will always be unlocked for you."

A matter of trust he didn't care to dwell on since he finally got her into his arms, looked for the door to the bedroom. "Residence, will you tell the Family, *our* Family, that we will be unavailable for the rest of the day and the evening and until morning—"

Something creaked rhythmically, the Residence sounding as if it made an amused cough-covering-laugh. That pleased him, too. He'd get along fine with this being. He strode to the bedroom, saw it looked like Enata, pretty. He tossed her on the bedsponge set in a fine, carved wooden platform.

"Clothes off." And, yeah, her eyes widened as she got a look at his condition and she flushed.

≈ Chapter 11 ≈

When they'd met, he'd wondered how far those flushes went down her body, had had a need to know. He'd found out—whole body flushes—but he wanted to see that again.

"Ahem," said the Residence. "I am banned from 'watching,' recording, or scanning bedrooms while they are being used for intimate associations."

That caused Barton to hesitate. "Uh, good?"

"So I wish to remind you both that Glyssa and Jace will be leaving for the site of the excavation of *Lugh's Spear,* a half a continent away, tomorrow morning before dawn. I respectfully request that I remind you both before dinner hour so you can attend a last meal with the travelers."

"Of course," Enata said. She'd rolled from the bed and her clothes fell away. All thought vanished from Barton's mind.

"Uh, sure," Barton said, forgetting what he was agreeing too. Some important Family thing, so, yeah, gotta do it. Duty.

"The Residence will ensure no one bothers us," Enata said.

"Absolutely."

Barton, took her hand, yanked her against him, and proceeded to pleasure her and himself until they fell shattering off the cliff of climax and into sleep.

Finally, they spent the rest of the day in bed, pleasing each other, talking in the sunlight, eating three *ritual meals* from her sitting room no-time. They munched down slices of furrabeast wrapped in thick bread from Yule that would take place a few months in the future. As usual, the no-time had kept the food the exact same temperature as it had gone into the unit.

By Yule the Licorices and the Clovers would celebrate the holiday together, as well as individually, Barton was sure. Hell, together they'd celebrate New Year, Samhain, just a little over two months away.

He and Enata ate a very quiet dinner with her Family. No echoing children's voices inside or outside the house. Barton had never had a dinner with his Family that didn't include children. Sort of restful, but something he didn't want to do more twice a week. He thought the Licorices would be stunned and wild-eyed at spending more than one dinner a week with the Clovers.

He liked the talk, though, Family matters, Family plans that appeared to make Jace more uncomfortable than Barton. When he found himself alone with Jace walking in the back grassyard, watching that man's hawkcel Fam fly, then circle and light upon his shoulder, Barton felt comfortable with him. After all, they both loved the Licorice daughters.

For sure, he felt more at ease with Jace Bayrum than T'Licorice. At least Barton had scraped up enough poetry to satisfy both parents.

Nope, he hadn't done too bad, but was really glad when they all retired to bed.

The next morning timer bells all around the house rang before dawn and everyone piled out of their rooms to say farewell to Glyssa and Jace. Enata seemed uncommonly fragile for some reason, so like

T'Licorice himself, Barton kept an arm around his wife's waist.

A couple of septhours later, Barton's calendar sphere sounded and pulled him and Enata from lazy drowsing.

"What?" Enata blinked sleepy eyes.

Propping himself onto his arm, he gazed at her, liking the looks of her in this bed more than his own. Yeah, he liked the atmosphere of this Residence just fine.

He pushed a tangle of hair from her face, let his calloused palm rest against her soft cheek. "Several people told me that we tend to be too serious."

She lifted to her elbow and the sight of her small breasts distracted him. He reached for a nipple. She batted his hand away and gave him a frown that didn't diminish the sparkle in her eyes. "Too serious?"

"Yeah, that." The clanging of the alarm from his calendar sphere reached ear-piercing levels. "I'm up," he shouted and it vanished with a pop.

Enata laughed and hopped out of bed. He admired her shapely thighs and nice ass. "You have a problem waking up."

"Sometimes," he muttered. "When I work too late the night before."

She nodded, walked to her wardrobe.

"Uh, too serious," he said. "Both of us. So I accepted GreatLady Danith D'Ash, the animal Healer's, invitation to a Fam Fair."

"A Fam Fair!" She whirled. Nice lean length, tidy breasts and curve of her hips, flat stomach.

He continued, "Danith is like an aunt to me, and

she's been wanting to match me up with a Familiar animal companion." He grimaced, especially when Enata drew on a robe and covered her beauty. "I think that was her solution to me working too hard. Anyway, the Fam Fair starts—" He glanced around the bedroom to see the wall timer, which he hadn't noticed before. "In about half a septhour." Clearing his throat, he said, "Wouldn't you like to go?"

A considering look came onto her face, then she nodded. "Yes."

"It's supposed to be fun."

She nodded again. "Fun." Then she flashed him a smile. "Not as fun as being in bed with you, but fun."

"Totally agree. How many Fams do the Licorices' have? I know of Glyssa's fox and Jace's bird."

He sensed her inner thoughts flinching and he regretted the question, though she answered easily.

"The first bird Fam on record. Neither my parents nor I have Fams. The PublicLibrary itself, as an intelligent being, has had two cat Fams for as long as I can remember." She paused. "They aren't particularly friendly."

"All right."

"What about the Clovers?" she asked. "What Fams does your Family have?"

"Trif Clover Winterberry, who lives in the compound with her husband and children, has a very persnickety FamCat. Her husband's FamFox is the alpha of the den on Clover land just outside the Compound. Walker has a fox and his wife has a housefluff, one of the Celtan mocyn-Earth rabbit hybrids. What about you, would you like a Fam?"

"Three days ago, before we met and wed, I'd have been thrilled. But now I have you, and all the connections coming at me from the Clovers. You're enough," she paused, caring eyes meeting his. "You're everything I've ever wanted for my lover and husband."

A hugeness of feeling, of tenderness and humility, of love, filled him, and tightened his throat so he couldn't speak. He rolled from bed and went to her, lifted her hand and kissed her fingers. "Why don't we go to the Fam Fair, see what happens? Not be results orientated in this. No expectations."

She raised their linked hands to her mouth and kissed his hand, smiled. "No expectations."

"We're good?" he couldn't prevent himself from asking.

"We're fabulous."

* * *

They arrived at the walled park hosting the Fam Fair just before the door in the gate opened. People—mostly nobles and dressed too well for interacting with animals—didn't queue but spread out along the street. He kept his hand under Enata's elbow. He liked staying physically connected with her. "It's by invitation only."

"Oh."

Then the door swung open and a large youngster in his mid-teens stood square in the opening. A young girl rushed forward, handed him her invitation, he stepped aside, and she hurried in. After that, everyone strolled in an orderly manner into the fair.

The young man gave him a papyrus map. "We

have about thirty Fams who decided to attend this Fair. Most of them are gathered together by type in an area or two . . . at least the pack and herd animals." He cleared his throat. "Watch out for cats in the tree branches overhead."

Barton and Enata laughed and moved down one of the winding gravel paths. His nose twitched at the multitude of smells. "From their scents I recognize foxes, cats, maybe even a dog or a horse or two."

"Oooh." Enata pressed against his side. "It will be fun."

They sauntered around, neither hurrying, enjoying the pleasant late summer's day. "I don't recall the last time I took a full day off and did . . . nothing."

She slipped her hand from his elbow to link fingers. "That's just sad, Barton."

"Yeah. I now have an excellent reason to keep my weekends free." He sent her a gentle leer.

They saw the girl who'd entered first holding a sweet-faced brown housefluff that she'd obviously bonded with. They smiled, walked over to the circular housefluff area—and all the Fams hurried to the far side.

"Huh," Barton said.

"They might have smelled the library cats on my clothes, and been afraid," Enata said.

"Fams know when other animal companions are intelligent. No eating is allowed," Barton stated. He thought about it. "In fact, I don't think I've even seen predatory Fams react that way to what would be, uh, prey in the wild."

Intelligent Fams do not smell or act like prey, said

a voice in his mind. Since Enata turned in the same direction as he, Barton figured she'd heard the Fam, too. A gray male wolf lounged under a big ash tree.

That sparked pure interest in Barton and he angled toward the Fam, projecting his thoughts, *Greetyou, FamWolf.*

The wolf met his eyes, *Greetyou, man.* His gaze slid to Enata and he dipped his head. *Greetyou woman who works in the place of knowledge.*

Greetyou, Enata replied with nearly as much enthusiasm as Barton himself.

When they were about three meters away, the wolf stood and said, *Stop!*

They did.

What's wrong? asked Barton.

Narrowing his eyes, the wolf stared at them, this time Enata first, then Barton, then the lupine turned his back. *I am not for you and you are not for me. Go away.*

Why? asked Barton and Enata, streaming the same word, as well as curiosity and hurt toward the wolf.

You are not good people to bond with.

Enata's shock echoed his own. His mind fizzed a little red, but she tucked her hurt and anger away and followed the line of questioning when he wouldn't have.

We ARE good people. We WOULD make good human Fam companions, she insisted.

With an impatient huff, the wolf glanced at them. *I did not question your characters. I said you wouldn't make a good bond.*

Is it because we are bonded with so many other

humans? Enata asked.

That is not a consideration, the wolf replied. *You smell odd. You the most, but the man, too.* Fur rippled down his spine like a human shrug. *The pattern of your vibrations are wrong, they will not allow for a harmonious bond to form. Probably not for you and any Fam companion at the moment,* the wolf ended trenchantly. *Go away and do not bother me.*

Since it looked as if the wolf would leave if they took another step toward him and Barton had moved through his irritation that the wolf had hurt Enata emotionally, he slipped his arm around her waist and they strolled to another enclosure.

This time two dogs sitting on pedestals stopped them and turned away. *Vibrations are wrong.*

So it went with the cats and foxes. They might not have spoken about vibrations, but none were interested in having Barton or Enata as a Fam companion.

This outing hadn't been as fun as he'd hoped. Especially when all around them animals and humans walked, or were carried, radiating delight at discovering a good Fam match.

Enata cleared her throat. "This is rather melancholy."

"I agree. I'd rather go back to bed."

She laughed and swung his hand. "Yes, let's. But it's a beautiful day, and this is a pleasant park, even if none of the Fams are ours, they're fun to watch. We don't have to hurry."

He beetled his brows at her. "No? It's been a while since we've loved."

"I'm sure that if we showed up at the Clover

Compound or D'Licorice Residence, we would be expected to be sociable and not just disappear into a bedroom. I am *so* looking forward to going back to a nosey Residence or Clover Compound." Her voice laced heavy with irony.

"You have a point."

Mewww. In their path sat a small ginger tabby kitten with one blue eye and one yellow eye.

≈ Chapter 12 ≈

When they looked at him, he rose to his back two paws and pawed the air with his front feet, claws extended. "Rrrrr." Then he sat back and looked inordinately pleased with himself.

Barton looked at his lover. "I think that was supposed to be a roar."

She laughed. "Perhaps."

He squatted down to look at the kitten, tugging on her hand and she followed him down but sat instead.

"Was that supposed to be a roar?" he asked the little triangular face pointed up at him.

It WAS a roar, the kitten affirmed. *You just did not hear all of it.* He sniffed. *It was not only in sounds that human ears can hear, but otherwise, TOO. And in the mind.* He flicked a forepaw. *See, EVERYONE heard My roar and is watching us.* Barton had felt focused attention, but looked around like Enata. For sure, everyone, animal and human, had turned in their direction.

"So, kitten—"

I am a CAT.

"You're a kitten," Enata said.

The tiny white-tipped tail, flicked, and small as he was, the kitten angled away from Enata and toward Barton. *This is a Fam Fair,* he said.

"Stating the obvious," Enata said, amusement in her voice.

Another miniscule sniff. I *am in the market for a FamMan.*

"What about all that bad vibrations stuff the other Fams told us about?" Barton asked, but he held out his hand—nearly bigger than the kitten—to the feline charmer. Like he'd said to Enata before they came, he'd had no expectations of getting a Fam. Since he'd—they'd—been here and been rejected, he'd revised his idea.

This time the cat's sniff was much louder. *I feel those icky vibrations, but they do not scare ME!*

Enata coughed.

Barton glanced over to her. Maybe it wouldn't be good to add another factor to the odd teeter-tottering balance of his new marriage. But . . . *What do you think?* he asked Enata telepathically.

She stood and brushed grass from her tunic. *I think this is one of those times when if you don't take this opportunity, you will always regret it.* She sounded indulgent.

The kitten leapt onto his hand, and Barton felt the prickle of claws on his palm, teeny teeth testing his thumb. "Then, I guess, I am also in the market for a FamKit—a FamCat."

ME!

"That's right."

I will sit on your head, the kitten said.

Barton snorted. "You think so?"

The kitten smiled ingratiatingly. *You are the biggest man here and the tallest and I want to SEE what the world is like from the top of your head.*

"He's got a point," Enata said aloud, smiling at him. He *loved* that carefree smile, and it had graced her face since the cat accosted them.

"All right. I will allow you to have your wish,"

Barton said to the kitten. "This once."

"You have lovely, thick hair," Enata murmured. "I like that it's long."

"It's not good in a fight," Barton said. "And Walker convinced me to follow that damn trend so we'd look more like those fashionable men of the older noble houses, so we'd blend in better."

She squeezed his biceps. "You will never blend in . . . unless it's with the Holly fighters."

"I worked for them," Barton said.

Me! Put Me on your head! the kitten demanded.

Keeping his neck solid, his head straight and still, Barton set the kitten on his head. Hoping he wasn't making a mistake.

"No terrible vibrations coming from me?"

Silly, the kitten said, *the vibrations come from the ground and through you and I am on your head. Much less. Oh, this is so FUN. I can see the WHOLE WORLD!* The little cat sounded thrilled. *I can see the stupid wolf, and over the wall to the street, and the houses beyond the park, and even THE STARSHIP, NUADA'S SWORD! I am SO high. My FamMan is SO tall. We own the world!*

A cat would think that.

Then the kitten sneezed in his hair. Barton grimaced and a rolling laugh broke from Enata.

Your hair smells good and is nice, the kitten said. *It tickled My nose.*

"It probably wouldn't have tickled your nose if you hadn't rooted that very nose around in it," Barton said between gritted teeth. "I think you're ready to come down."

Noooo!

"I think we're ready to leave the park," Enata said matter-of-factly. "I'll teleport us to D'Licorice Residence." She slanted Barton a look and he nodded. "I'm fine with staying another night in the relative peace and quiet of D'Licorice Residence."

"Less relatives, more peace and quiet," she agreed. Her head angled as she looked at the cat. "D'Licorice Residence doesn't have a Fam living within its walls . . . yet." Another pause. "Hmmm. I wouldn't feel safe teleporting with a kit—cat on Barton's head."

I need to come down now. I will jump all the way down to your shoulder!

And he sailed off Barton's head. Barton barely felt the weight of him as the cat landed on his shoulder.

And here We are! the kitten said as he settled along Barton's shoulder. The small cat began to purr.

"You have a nice purr." Enata moved toward Barton's other side, close to the kitten, and took Barton's hand in her own.

I know, the kitten said.

They'd reached the path straight to the door in the wall when a woman hustled up to them—GreatLady Danith D'Ash, a woman like an aunt to Barton. Her whole body shimmied as she saw the tiny kitten with bi-colored eyes. "I see you and the youngest tom have bonded. He is a wonderful Fam for a young married couple."

Barton slanted her a wry look. "As if I don't have enough children in my Family I can practice on."

"They aren't living with you, are they?" D'Ash asked. "Taking care of a young thing, together—"

She nodded. "Yes, this is right for you."

"Thank you," he said politely.

"What are you going to name him?"

The kitten hopped on his shoulder with claws a little too flexed for Barton's comfort. *Yes, yes, what IS My name?*

"I think I'll call you, Resup, a good Clover name."

"Very nice," Enata murmured.

I like Resup. From the pinnacle of Barton's shoulder, he lowered his head and sneered at Danith D'Ash. *It is much better than Youngest Tom.*

Danith's smile strained.

Let's go to D'Licorice Residence! Resup trilled.

Barton stopped in his tracks. He'd been thinking of spending the rest of the day in bed with Enata. Now he had a kitten to care for. They had a kitten to care for.

With a sigh, he met Danith's eyes. "He's on a two septhour feeding schedule, right?"

She smiled. "That's right."

"He's a treasure," Enata said. She held out tentative fingers to the kitten who licked them, then she stroked him—the cat, not Barton.

"So very soft."

Well, yeah, Barton didn't have much softness about him. Except his big gooey heart for his woman and wife, and the little scrap of fur riding on his shoulder. Somehow he had to make sure that he stayed in charge.

* * *

Luckily the kitten ran out of energy quicker than he and Enata. Playing with Resup turned into an intimate bonding experience among the three of them as they practiced their telepathy, and simply lowered their emotional shields to be vulnerable.

Enata's parents returned home earlier than WorkEnd Bell, which he understood to be unusual. Soon enough he realized they missed their other daughter and wanted to spend time with Enata—who would mostly reside with him at Clover Compound when off work. As he watched the Licorices, Barton decided that he should stay here some nights each week.

He could set that up, train others and delegate more. Good for his security force. That sounded reasonable but the idea of giving up the reins of control made his fingers twitch.

The kitten, when he awoke, proved to be exceedingly amusing and distracting for the older Licorices and the evening passed in good cheer until it was time to retire.

Once upstairs, Enata cleared out an alcove with a window seat in her sitting room for Resup's very own personal space. The kitten hopped all around the blue velvet cushion roaring . . . squeaking . . . with excitement.

Barton stuffed his new Fam full of food and liquid and left the kitten curled up in his window. Next to that window was a small, new, pet no-time that would help with dispensing meals; a litter box sat with the toilets.

He pulled the door to the bedroom closed to a crack that Resup could shove through if he wanted it enough, then led Enata to bed.

In the soft twinmoons light he undressed her, this time piece by piece. First he traced his index finger along her shoulder, just to feel the lines of it. Then he trailed it again, this time he separated the shoulder tab so the top of her tunic opened. He repeated the gesture on her left shoulder, then peeled her top down to her waist, exposing the delicacy of her body.

Now he used his thumbs to smooth over her fine collarbones, from shoulder to the dip. So very elegant and beautiful.

Her breastband, a swatch of white lace over her equally exquisite small breasts, showcased her subtle curves and the deep pink tips. His mouth went dry and his sex instantly thickened.

He sucked in a breath to keep the lust-fog from removing all thought from his mind. Fading back a step, then two, he gazed at her, standing in a stream of moonslight. Just fabulous.

After a hard swallow, he went to her, stripped away her tunic and threw it aside, touched the top of the seams of her trous at her hips, heard the soft whoosh as the trous opened and fell.

Placing his hands around her waist, he lifted her from the pool of material, angled her in the moonslight so she became an even more fascinating woman of light and shadows, like she was both tart and sweet.

Her pantlettes sat low on her stomach and rose high on her legs, another mere scrap barely shielding secrets that could drive a man mad—him mad. He drew his hands up her torso, plumping her breasts. He wanted to see how those breasts, those hard berry nipples, looked wet from his tongue. How the lace might pattern them.

His shaft grew harder, thicker. Control shredded. But he needed it, with this woman, his wife. He had to keep her. Keep her drugged with the same pleasure that pervaded him when they came together.

He bent his head to lap one nipple.

She gasped, and her head fell back as she arched into him. He set his teeth on the nub, did nothing else. Just let her feel the contrast between teeth, then tongue, then the moving of damp lace over her sensitive skin. Her body trembled against him, rubbing his shaft.

With languid grace, as if her arms felt heavy, she put her arms around his neck, and her fingers slipped under his hair at the nape.

Her gaze met his, her eyes glassy. "Barton," she sighed, pressed against him and rubbed, her fingers toying with his hair.

His control broke. His fingers ripped away her pantlettes. He took three paces to a silkeen-covered wall and braced her against it, hands on the globes of her ass.

"Clothes off!" he commanded and they dropped from him and the next instant he thrust inside her.

Her tight, wet heat welcomed him. "Barton," she gasped.

How sweet, how incredible, moving in her, the slide of friction, the race to the climax, sped on by her sex noises. Long strokes. Extend the pleasure. Pause as long as he could at her entrance until she begged, until the ecstasy beckoning couldn't be denied. Plunge in. Rock.

Listen to her scream, then triumph as she

shuddered around him and his own release roared through him.

Stumble to bed, fall on it, hold her close as sweet darkness closed over him.

* * *

Floral fragrance drifted through her dreams, turning sparkle and joyful glitter into dark shards of obsidian glass that fell and sliced bits of herself away and gone. An imperative order wrapped around her, demanded her attention.

≈ Chapter 13 ≈

Enata awoke deep in the night, body and heart heavy and sluggish.

Lady and Lord, the scent of honeysuckle called to her, triggered a desperate need in her that had nothing to do with sex, but did promise some sort of easing of the awful ache inside her she'd experienced all month.

She slipped from bed, drew on a robe, a real professional Librarian robe, and walked toward the door.

"Spell globes on," Barton said. Light brightened the bedroom. "Where are you going?" he asked.

Caught! She closed her eyes, hesitated, then opened them and turned back. He lay against the pillows, his muscular arms behind his head, staring at her, his expression neutral.

"Not to a lover." Her voice cracked.

He jerked, then stiffened as if his body had betrayed him.

"I've had no other lover than you in the . . ." She swallowed as she numbered the days, "nearly a full year."

His dark blue gaze didn't waver. She let her shoulder drop and rubbed her face, crossed to perch on the end of the bed. "I suppose I should tell someone what's happening."

"You can trust me, always, Enata." He assured her with an intense gaze.

She turned to fully face him. They met and matched stares, and she strove to look beyond the attractive male, lowered her eyelids and tilted her head to *listen* to the bond between them, feel it. Strong and reliable.

This man took the welfare of his Family personally. He cared for them.

And he cared for her. He just . . . overwhelmed her . . . and not simply him, but his Family. Like a tidal wash, grabbing her into an undertow where she'd lose herself. She set her stance and wariness came into his eyes.

"I'm very sorry I ran."

He sat up and made a cutting gesture. "That's past and not important."

She stood as restlessness along her nerves. Swallowing, and keeping her eyes matched with his, she said, "I've felt—off—since the beginning of the month, new twinmoons." She shook out her body. "When I wake in the morning, I'm tired as if I didn't sleep well."

"You should see a Healer," he stated, leaning over and grabbing her though she'd thought she was beyond his reach, and plunking her on his lap. For the moment she ignored the more interesting condition of his body to focus on the morass of her mind.

A man of action. Take charge. Of course he would want to fix the problem. "I did. I moved my annual health check up a few months. They found nothing. I told them about the headaches and they said nothing seemed very unusual."

One big arm wrapped around her and she let herself slump into his strong embrace.

"Nothing very unusual?"

Sniffling, she pulled a softleaf from her sleeve

pocket. "They said that my work must be challenging because my mind had more neural connections than the last map they'd done." Enata blew her nose. "But Healers, even Mind Healers, rather expect that of us Librarians and, ah, other scholars."

Barton squeezed her until she squeaked and looked him in his eyes, his gaze holding amusement. "As opposed to fighters and Chiefs of Security where they'd expect our muscles to expand more than our brains."

"I suppose." Frowning, she said, "And once I met with priestess Tiana Mugwort. I didn't know what to say. So I pulled out a sheet of papyrus from my sleeve and read it to her." Enata drew in a breath. "I was wearing this robe. I think I've been wearing this robe quite a lot, lately."

"It's a pretty gown. I like the blue-green on you."

She nodded and reached into the opposite rectangular sleeve pocket and extracted the same piece of papyrus, handed it to Barton and they perused it together. *I have something of great importance that I must remember, and occasionally I do, but usually I forget. As I have now. It is not a Healer problem, it is a spiritual problem.*

"And the priestess couldn't help you?"

Enata shrugged. "I attended a few more rituals. Nothing helped." She wriggled on his lap, felt the stirring of his sex. "I'm sorry, I've got to leave. I must—"

"Must go," he said, consideringly. "I sensed a darkness in you."

"A darkness in me!" she cried.

"Shhh. We don't want to wake Resup. Didn't we

just feed him a quarter septhour ago?"

"Did we?"

"I did. Let the kitten sleep."

"Yes. I don't think this is a matter for kittens." She bit her lip and her voice broke on her next words. "You felt a darkness in me?"

"A smudge, like from a trauma."

She shifted again. "I've got to go."

"Let's see where." To her extreme surprise he threw her into the air, so far she could have touched the ceiling, hopped from the bed and caught her easily when she plummeted down. She did note that his erection had subsided, too bad.

"I'll dress," he said and strode to the closet she didn't use because she preferred a wardrobe. When he slid open the door, she saw a space full of his clothes, and she didn't know when that happened. He dressed quickly in a tunic-trous outfit as professional as hers. Then he whirled and demanded, "Where do you go, Enata?"

"To Secure Vault One," she answered automatically, then gasped.

He nodded. "So your unconscious has some knowledge of what is happening to you. We just need to mine it."

"Agreed."

"I think we should take a look at this vault of yours."

Yes, a man who'd work at a problem until he solved it.

"You're coming, too?"

"You aren't alone anymore, Enata. Not struggling with this alone."

Tears pressed behind her eyes, then she blurted out another thought. "That vault has our most important items. The most ancient of all our records, some from Earth and the first generation on Celta."

He slanted a narrowed-eyed look at her. "What, I'm not allowed in?"

She hesitated. "You're not a scholar." Then she lifted her chin. "But you are a member of the Family." Clearing her throat from her previous tears—so emotional lately, too!—she added, "And you're honorable. Strong and honorable."

He bowed to her as if she was a FirstFamily GreatLady, then raised a brow. "I will also remind you that I am the Chief of Security for a large Family."

"So you are accustomed to keeping secrets?"

"That's right." He took her hand and placed it in the corner of his elbow. Optimism flowed from him through their link. He had no doubts that they'd discover the problem and remedy the matter. A relieved sigh escaped her. She'd had little buoyancy in her life lately that didn't include Barton. She'd work on that. But for now, she managed a spring in her step.

Until they reached the threshold of the bedroom. Barton doused the light. "We'll tiptoe past the kitten."

"I could teleport us," she whispered.

He hesitated, then she felt him shake his head. "No. That takes strength and Flair, and something has been hurting you." His tone took on a note of iron. "We may need all the strength and Flair we have when we discover what we battle."

Hand in hand, they made it out of her rooms,

though she thought the Residence must mark their journey, then through the tunnel to the basement of the PublicLibrary and the oldest and strongest part of the foundation that held Secure Vault One. She opened the round door and they stepped inside.

Barton sniffed, loudly. "Nice smell. Flatsweets. With cocoa chips."

She stared. "The vault is filled with a strong honeysuckle scent."

Emotions flowed through his eyes that she couldn't decipher, then he revealed softly, "The smell of cocoa chip flatsweets means love to me. My mother made them for me when I got the apprenticeship to The Green Knight Fencing and Fighting Salon, when I reached my journeyman and master levels, when the Hollys asked me to stay on as an instructor." He let out a breath and drew another. "So she made them every time she was particularly proud of me. Or when I broke a bone or was sick, when I came back from the Healer. When I needed comfort, as well." His gaze drilled into hers. "What does honeysuckle mean to you?"

"Oh." She coughed. "You know that each of us, Mother and Father and Glyssa—" another hesitation and a hurt she didn't understand but had her frowning.

"Enata, lo—, wife?" Barton prompted.

She focused. "We each have our own library in the Residence. Mine smells of honeysuckle. My mother's father, MotherSire, whom I never knew, came from the Honeysuckle Family. Honeysuckle does mean love to me. At least it did before the beginning of the month, two weeks and four days ago." she shook her head. "Now I don't care for the smell so much."

"Let me guess," Barton said dryly. "Your MotherSire Honeysuckle was a scholar."

"He studied the preservation of records, wrote the definitive monograph on it, and we still use his methods today. With his processes, we should be able to ensure our papyrus and books, vizes and recordspheres, will last millennia."

Barton squeezed her fingers. "Good work, then. Speaking of books," he angled his chin. "That one is glowing blue green and shooting off silver sparks. Is that normal?"

She looked up to see a volume straight ahead, in the middle of the shelf, glowing yellow and the spine running with silver and gold sparks.

The door behind them closed with a solid thunk and an equally loud clack as the large lock rotated. She murmured, "The door is not bespelled to shut and neither you nor I closed it."

Barton smiled and his voice came even more quietly than hers. "A little creepy."

Curiosity slid through their bond, along with his excitement. The notion they were making progress.

With a gulp, and straightening her shoulders, no more cowardice in her life, she walked to the shelf and touched the wide book spine. Tingles ran from her fingers through her body. She jerked a little and gasped. And Barton was there, yanking the book out.

"Cave of the Dark Goddess!" he cursed, then simply let go of the large volume and shook out his fingers.

The book didn't fall, but floated on an anti-grav

spell, then it opened and thick papyrus pages flipped. Barton wrapped his arm around her waist and the brawn of it, the steadiness of their shared feelings, kept her own emotions stable.

They stepped to stare at the book together.

Looking up at her, with a wide smile, was her brother. "Reglis Landu Licorice," she read aloud in a choked voice. "CHOSEN," she nearly shouted. She'd read those words so often before. "I remember!" Her body began to shake and she wrapped her arms around herself. "Now I remember. All the times I've been in here this month!"

Barton turned her into his body, but his gaze remained on the book. "You never mentioned a brother." He cleared his throat. "None of you Licorices mentioned that there was a third child, an older brother to you and Glyssa."

"Because we don't remember!" Enata nearly screamed, her hysterical words echoed in the vault and made her compose herself. "None of us remember." Pressing her hands together, she calmed herself, as she had also done many times before. She'd come to the vault nearly every night, only skipping the last two nights because of her marriage. "At least I don't remember until I'm back here in the vault, reading this volume."

"What's the title of this book?"

"I don't know. There is nothing inscribed on the spine or the front cover. I don't recall reading the title page."

"Chosen," Barton repeated. "Any Clovers in here?"

"I don't think so." Holding her breath, she

struggled to turn a page back from the entry on her brother, toward the front of the book, biting her lip until it hurt, feeling the muscles in her neck turn tight, she said, "It isn't often that I can move the pages." One flipped over. "Corylus Hazel." Another sheet. She held her breath. "Calluna Heather Hazel." She swallowed and read aloud, "'HeartMates acquired in the year noted as 405 years after the Colonization of Celta.'"

"405," Barton said. "The previous . . . chosen . . . before your brother left sixteen years ago. When did your brother . . . disappear?"

Enata spoke through a clogged throat. "Earlier this year, in the spring." Her lips trembled. "Reglis," she moaned his name.

Her fingers slipped and the papyrus sliced her—a deep paper cut—and blood slowly welled to the top of her skin.

"This is hurting you, more than emotionally, physically, too." He picked her up. "We're getting out of here." He turned toward the entrance of the vault.

A filthy headache struck, along with a tense, upset stomach and she allowed herself to go limp in Barton's arms, glad he held her. "Open the door," he snapped.

Croaking a spell couplet she waved the thick vault door open and Barton carried her out of the place.

He lowered her to her feet, stuck his arm stiff against the wall next to the closed door of the vault, as if propping himself up. Several minutes passed in panting silence, then Barton stated, "We came here because you were compelled."

"Yes," she whispered, both her hands going to knead the back of her neck, trying to loosen stiff muscles.

"We went into the vault," he said flatly.

Giving up on her neck, she rubbed her temples. "I think so." Then she stretched long and hard. For the first time since they'd been together, his eyes didn't follow her movements.

"We should return to bed," she said weakly.

But he shook his head, rather like a bull, turned and squinted at the closed and solid vault door. "It got me, too, didn't it?"

"What?"

"You can't remember being in there just a little while ago, can you?"

She hesitated, then shook her head. "No."

"It got me, too. I can't remember."

≈ Chapter 14 ≈

"We left for a reason," she pointed out, dreading the thought of returning.

"Let's go back in." He took a step, wobbled, and the muscles in his jaw bunched with teeth-set determination.

She stepped back so she could see all of his tall form, crossed her arms and studied him.

"You have a headache."

"Oh, yeah. Like hammers hitting my skull—inside and out." He winced, wiped a hand across his eyes and she saw perspiration coated his skin. "My gut feels bad, too." He looked at the vault and snarled. "We *will* do this. Find out what is affecting you *and* me. Maybe any Licorice that comes into the vault, maybe any Librarian. You got any records as to who's accessed this vault since the beginning of the month?"

A veil of sickness seemed to separate her from the rest of the world, but she concentrated on his question. "Yes, upstairs in the library, but I don't think I have the strength to translocate that."

"We'll look at it later." His mouth set, and the hand he held out trembled. "This is a matter that *must* be handled, and we can do it, together."

"Yes, together." She took his hand and they entered the vault.

Four minutes later they stared at the floating volume.

"Reglis Licorice," Barton stated. "Corylus Hazel, Calluna Heather Hazel, HeartMates. All 'acquired.' Vanished from Druida City . . ."

"Vanished from memories," Enata said, voice thick.

"Wait!" Barton's eyes lit. "Wait." He sounded excited.

"What?"

His fingers fisted, then released. "My two relations are missing with no trace of them. I know all of these people have been nobles, but we Clovers are nobles, now. Do you think—"

"Perhaps."

He jerked a nod at the volume. "Let's look."

Drawing in a deep breath, she held it, counted a few seconds and released it. "Yes. We can do that."

Carefully, she turned the page away from the picture of her smiling brother, from the biography of his life and his list of skills, to the next page, placed her fingers on another sheet, folded it over. "Savi Clover, CHOSEN." She gasped and Barton swore, vilely.

Then he met her eyes. "It only says Savi."

"Yes."

"Then what happens to Balansa?"

"I don't know." Two fat tears rolled from her eyes. "When we leave this vault, we'll forget again, as everyone else has forgotten. Every time I leave, I've forgotten." The realization struck her so that she leaned over, hands on knees, shaking. Barton put his arm around her, raised her and she turned naturally into him. "Even D'Licorice HouseHeart has forgotten!" Needing to explain, even in this distress, words punctuated her sobs. "I was in the HouseHeart before our marriage two days ago and it talked about me becoming D'Licorice!"

"May your mother live a long, long life," Barton said fervently, with a note of humor in his voice that she cherished. This—him holding her, being tender with her, caring for her, showed she hadn't bungled their relationship too badly. He stroked her back and she wrapped her arms around his waist, hugging close, then whispered, "What force could do that? Bespell all of our memories, even a HouseHeart's?"

"I don't know." His voice sounded hard. He took her wrists and moved a half-step away, touched under her chin and she looked up at him. "I don't know what person or monster could do, would do, such a terrible thing that hurt so many. But we will find out. For your brother and my cuzes."

She inclined her head. "Yes. For our loved ones."

He frowned, heavy brows dipping and she touched the line between his eyes, the soft skin there. "What?" she asked, sensing he thought of something else.

Slowly, he reeled out words as if he weighed an idea behind each one. "I have been fixated on Savi and Balansa. Even when Walker ordered me to leave the investigation alone, let them go, I could *not*. I've been obsessed." His body jerked in an explosive breath. "I didn't know them, lived on the far side of the compound than them. I concentrated on my immediate family, my guards, other charges. Didn't paid any attention to Savi and Balansa—not enough attention, and that was our failure. That failure ate at me."

"And you think that might be another spell?"

"Maybe." He drew her close again, one arm around her, and they turned to watch the book still bobbing mid-air. "Or maybe there was the beginning of that compulsion to forget." With his free hand, he rubbed his temple. "Now that I think about it, I believe I can sense tendrils of forgetfulness softening my memories." His mouth quirked. "Maybe I'm just contrary and rebellious and fighting such a constraint."

A shiver trembled through Enata. "I *hate* being manipulated."

"Ah," Barton said, turned to face her, and kept his arms loosely around her waist. More tenderness flowed from him. "Yeah, we Clovers tend to have certain ideas and expectations of our Family members. The women did try to roll over you. I assure you that won't happen again."

"I won't let that happen again. Nor will I let your uncle Pink or your brother Walker dictate my place in your Family. I will make my own place."

Barton squeezed her. "Good."

She slid her hands up his chest, loving the feel of smooth skin over tough muscle under her palms. "I won't leave again, and I won't let you go."

His eyelids dropped over a glinting gaze, "I won't let you go, either. You are mine forever."

Her knees weakened, especially since a huge surge of love accompanied those words.

Then, with a sigh, they moved in unison to the book.

He glared down at the volume. Flicked a finger at it. "This bio info is all well and good, but where *are* they?"

She inhaled, closed her eyes and rubbed her temples, thinking. "Whatever has bespelled this tome hasn't let me move beyond the biographies."

"Yet," he growled. His jaw flexed, then he sent a sideways glance at her. "You've been in here often this month."

"Yes, nearly every night." Her voice caught. "And always I forget, then remember. It's horrible."

"It would be. But you learn a little more each time?"

"Yes. If I stay here long enough, I can move through the book. I can read all of the entries, now."

His eyes narrowed and his smile went sly. "Maybe it's a puzzle to be solved. The more often you come, and use it, the more you discover about it, you are rewarded."

"Perhaps," she said doubtfully, touched the thick pages stuck together at the back. "There should be an index back here."

"And a title page, too. What else do you know about this book?"

"I don't know."

"Think, FirstLevel Librarian."

"The cover," she finally said. "We know about the cover, and that gives us a clue to where the lost ones are!" She barely moved her fingers aside before Barton snapped the book shut. They stared at the dark blue leather cover. He touched the front. "Not furrabeast leather."

Enata shrugged, then tapped with her silver and gold nails on the outline of the map, the island off the coast. "This place is not on any other map of Celta. Not one." Her voice lowered. "The very first time I saw this volume, I'd been sent to retrieve the first copies of the maps taken by the starship *Nuada's*

Sword as it entered our atmosphere, circled the planet and landed." Her finger shook. "This island isn't on those maps." She scooted over to a viz sphere, took it, set it in the air and tapped the glass to project a huge globe. They stared at the unblemished sea off the coast of the peninsula holding Druida City, then they looked at the book, with a map of the island.

"The last I heard of my cuzes was that they were at the docks. They'd taken a ship heading west." He rubbed his temples with thumb and forefinger. "Savi and Balansa are gone, but we haven't forgotten them, yet. Not me, nor Walker nor any of the other Clovers." He glanced at her. "What does that mean?"

"I don't know."

"We've been here long enough. The air in here is turning odd."

"If we leave, we'll forget."

"Will we? Something . . . someone wanted you to find this book. Has instilled compulsion in you and obsession in me. Now we've figured out about the Chosen, and where they might be. Maybe that's enough. I hope so." He tapped the globe and handed the viz back to her, took the closed book and pulled. Nothing happened. He let go, loosened his shoulder and back muscles, grabbed the book again and dragged with a steady pressure and enough effort that Enata saw all the muscles bunch under his tunic. The book didn't move.

Finally, as sweat dampened his back, he swore and gave up, glanced at Enata. "Well, we can't take it with us. Do you have a writestick?"

She went to a box of supplies and pulled one out.

He shoved up his sleeve and wrote with thick strokes on his inner arm: *Remember? No? Go in vault.*

"I think I tried that," she said.

He shrugged. "We'll continue this *research* until we can fix the problem. Ready?" He offered his hand.

Enata linked fingers with him. Barton dropped the marker in a box on the way out, Enata opened the door and they left.

≈ Chapter 15 ≈

Once outside the vault, Enata closed the door, giving Barton the spellwords to open it. They sank down to sit leaning against the round metal wall of the door, cold against their backs.

"You still remember your brother?" he demanded.

She turned with raised brows. "The fact that you recall my brother means the forgetfulness spell isn't working." She blinked and an expression of wonder came to her eyes. "And I don't feel too bad. No headache or nausea!" Blowing out a breath and inhaling, matching their breathing, they stared at each other.

"Such potent spells." A line appeared between her brows, as if she considered the puzzling circumstances. "Affecting both of us."

He took her hand and kissed it. "You are extraordinary. To have battled this every night, to lose your memory, feel so ill... yet still continue. I am awed by your courage."

She gave him a crooked smile, one side of her mouth up, the rest flat. "A compulsion worked upon me. I had no choice."

"I think you did," he said slowly. "If you really wanted to destroy that volume, for instance, I think you could. If you wanted to walk away from this vault and refuse to enter it ever again, I think that would be possible, too. You're a fighter, like me. And you solve puzzles, too. Like me."

"We can do this together." She repeated his

words simply.

"Track our loved ones and find them and *talk* to them," he said.

"Make sure they are all right and," her voice thickened, "happy."

"And we know where to go."

"We know where to go." She flung herself into his arms and he held her close.

They stayed, embracing in the basement of the PublicLibrary, for long minutes. *Now* Enata could feel the bond with her brother! As if it had been blocked. Blessed bond. Even if her parents didn't recall it, or Glyssa—yet—Enata felt it. Her beloved brother Reglis.

FamMan, where are you! whined a tiny, insistent voice. *I want you to feed Me. I want you to pet Me. I want to sit on your head.*

Barton chortled, stood and hauled her up, then twined his fingers with hers. *We are coming.*

They walked toward the tunnel to D'Licorice Residence and she staggered only a little more than her very physically fit lover. The time in Secure Vault One had been hard on them.

"All that crap about vibrations," Barton said thoughtfully. "Worse in you, but also in me. The compulsion and obsession."

She shivered and put her thoughts into solid words. "Who, or what, has the power to wipe clean the memories of everyone? Who or what can stop us from feeling the primal link of a sibling bond?"

Barton's expression went grim.

"We'll find out."

* * *

But it took two full days of both of them using all their sources before they got results. Enata asked all the librarians and perused the book in the vault time and again. Barton tugged on all his contacts from GreatLord Straif T'Blackthorn, the noted tracker and his cuz Mitchella's husband, to Garrett Primross, a private investigator. Finally a grubby anonymous note came to them—to Enata at D'Licorice Residence one evening—that was written in very old script with instructions. *If you want more information on the Chosen, you and the Clover and the Clover's FamCat show up at Pier twenty-three tomorrow at NoonBell for a sail to Cyfrinach Island. Not a moment sooner. No more than half a septhour later. Look for the ship Lady of Celta and Captain M. Mor.*

Barton nipped the note from Enata's fingers and squinted at the handwriting, grunted. They'd remained off work and stayed at D'Licorice Residence. The multitude of the Clover bonds continued to bother Enata and being at her home mitigated that.

Besides, he didn't want anyone, like his brother, to realize they had ulterior motives in planning a wedding trip. Resup the kitten, of course, was thrilled he'd be traveling, then quite dubious when they went to the beach and watched the rolling surf. But he stuck with Barton, would not be left behind.

"Captain M. Mor," Enata murmured. "Another FirstFamily, Mor. There was a Manan Mor *Chosen* twenty-five years ago."

"The current FirstFamily GrandLady D'Mor practices the Family profession of mind Healing," Barton added. He and Enata shared a bleak look.

They'd both come to the conclusion that when the memories of a Chosen was excised, it harmed all the individuals of a Family, as well as the Family itself, not to mention the Residence. That had been another creepy discovery. Though they spoke openly about the Chosen and the book, *The Chosen of Celta*, and the Residence knew their plans, when casually asked about Reglis, D'Licorice Residence didn't recall who he was.

Nor did anyone else, and now melancholy lived in Enata's eyes that not even kitten antics could banish.

And Barton didn't want his Family losing memories and fracturing.

They had determined that no one else had had ill effects from visiting Secure Vault One;, that had been confined to Enata and him.

So they packed that day, and discussed their plans, then they went first to his Family since they anticipated they'd be the easier to break the news to. And so it proved.

The Clover elders at home had welcomed them, listened to their carefully shaded prevarications and smiled with smug indulgence while giving them dispensation to leave.

Barton didn't think that even his parents, Walker, or Walker's wife Sedwy, a noted behavioral observer, realized that he and Enata weren't being completely truthful.

Nor had Barton's second in command in the guards, or any of the security staff, which was a little disappointing.

That evening after dinner, they tackled the

Licorices during Family time in the sitting room.

"We intend to take a wedding trip," Enata said.

D'Licorice's face went expressionless, worse, her eyes blank. She slumped in her wing chair. "Leave? Leave us alone in this Residence. All by ourselves? We've never lived all by ourselves." She turned and reached out to her HeartMate, groped for the hand that he gave her, then tightened her fingers as he did the same.

T'Licorice got up from his seat, bent to his wife and kissed her cheek, sat on the arm of her chair. "Having a newly wed couple take a trip is a common enough event, dearest. And we have each other."

"We'll be alone."

A rich chuckle from her husband. "That isn't necessarily bad, my love."

"I don't think I can, Fasic." Her voice rose.

"Ah, Rhiza." He gathered her into his arms. "Dearest, instead of staying in an empty Residence, why don't *we* take a small vacation, too, perhaps to our house in Gael City we haven't visited for three years. Or we could stay with my Family, the Almonds. They have plenty of space."

"What of the Residence? It might think we are abandoning—"

"Not at all," the Residence said. "I am not so shallow. And . . ." A long creaking came as if from floorboards, "I have wanted to do some internal renovations, moving walls and such. I have plenty of gilt in my budget for construction, and I have learned it's best if humans aren't around during such a time. I intend to make a suite for GrandSir Clover next to Enata's, with an office. Rework the craft room in the basement for better use by Jace Bayrum when he and Glyssa stay with us—"

"They aren't coming back!" Enata's mother broke down, turning to her husband. "They are staying in that dangerous and savage place!"

Barton noticed the whole atmosphere warmed around them and a subtle smell of soothing herbs released into the air. Very interesting.

"I don't believe that to be true," the Residence said. "I am older than all you humans. I have my knowledge of people, the combined wisdom of my fellow Residences and that of the starship, *and* access to all PublicLibrary files. I doubt the camp at the excavation of *Lugh's Spear* can be physically turned into a permanent community in the next half decade. That means Glyssa and Jace Bayrum will most likely winter here in Druida City."

"Oh," D'Licorice sniffled.

Barton took the opportunity to say, "You will always be welcome at the Clovers. Be given your own suite or even a small house. I guarantee you that you can be as busy and sociable there as you'd ever wish."

Two pairs of Licorice eyes stared at him. Enata's mother's mouth actually hung open in surprise.

"Maybe a trip to the Gael City house would be good," D'Licorice said. Then she disentangled herself from her husband, stood, and curtseyed to Barton. "We thank you very much for your generous offer, and I'm sure that as we become more acquainted with your Family we will take you up on that offer in the future."

Enata hugged her mother, held out her arm so

her father could join their Family embrace. "I will always be here for you," she said, and Barton could hear she meant it, and that it comforted her Family, even though that wasn't a promise she could control. "I am not abandoning you, mother, father. I simply wish to spend time with my husband—as I know each of you cherishes the time you spend alone with each other."

The three heads dipped together until they touched, arms linked in a loose circle, and the hum of private Family thought, maybe even including the Residence, impinged on Barton's senses. He was outside, but didn't feel slighted. Instead he watched the Family dynamic.

He figured that Enata had changed her relationship with her parents, altered the way they would see her, interact with her, in the future.

They'd no longer have the command of her that they'd had. She'd take their feelings into consideration, but she wouldn't be ruled by them. This would slop over into their careers as FirstLevel Librarians, the Family business. The elder Licorices could no longer dictate to Enata what she would do. And Barton didn't think she'd maintain as cool a professional exterior as she had in the past, not his warm woman who began to bloom on her own.

He'd helped her with that, and he was proud to know he'd contributed, even knowing that his own battles with his Family, and perhaps hers, too, lay ahead. After they finished this wedding trip.

≈ Chapter 16 ≈

The next day, an hour before NoonBell, Barton and Enata ate brunch in the main kitchen of Clover Compound to say a casual goodbye to his relatives. He didn't really anticipate anything going wrong, but who knew? Bottom line, they were dealing with someone or something that could rip the memories from every member of a Family. So he updated his will and left it with Walker.

With one last glance around his near sterile bedroom, he picked up his bag as Enata did hers. Resup, full of food, slept inside Barton's duffle.

She smiled, looking a whole lot more comfortable than the last time she was here, good. The whole Family had given her room, and Barton had made sure that other professional women had been at lunch—his cuz Trif and Walker's HeartMate, Sedwy.

"Ready?" Enata asked, a lilt in her voice.

Excitement zipped through him, too. "Yeah." Clearing his throat, he said, "You know the Family thinks of this as a starter house for a bachelor since there's only two bedrooms. Would you like something . . . more?"

Chuckling, she shrugged. He saw no opinion in her eyes as she said, "You'll also be living in a connecting suite in D'Licorice Residence. We share that Residence with my parents." She dropped her bag and held out her hands. He walked up and took them, felt the strong bond between them.

She said, "It matters that I'm with you. I—we—don't know the future, how many children we might have. I am fine with any living arrangement as long as we're together."

He kept his expression serious, then sent a final spurt of telepathy to his brother Walker. *We are leaving now!*

Have a great time! Walker replied mentally.

I intend to.

Better you than me on the ocean, Walker sent absently, then Barton felt his mind focus on a task. Barton let out a breath. Looked like he and Enata had escaped detection absolutely clean.

Time to teleport. He moved behind his wife, wrapped his arm around her waist, brought her up against him. He loved keeping her in his arms, being with her, more every day. "Come on," he murmured, "Let's head out, count us down." He nuzzled her ear.

"You're very distracting."

He laughed. "So are you. It's all good, I think . . . I feel . . . I believe."

"We'll 'port to pier nineteen, outside a branch library."

"Fine."

A few minutes later a cool ocean breeze whipped at their clothes. "Fall Equinox, Mabon holiday in a couple of weeks," Barton said, folding his fingers over her cold ones. "I don't want to celebrate without Savi and Balansa."

She touched his cheek with her free hand and he looked into her eyes. "Barton, those people in *The Chosen of Celta,* Manan Mor, Corylus Hazel, Colluna Heather Hazel, and Reglis . . . they could have returned here if they wanted. You must accept that."

"As you've accepted it?"

"I sense my bond with my brother, and he's . . .

content." She brought their linked hands to her breasts and he felt the thump of her heart. "No matter what, I must be happy with his choice, just as I must be pleased with Glyssa's to live across the continent. *Their* choice. What fulfills *them*. My choice for them and my needs about them must not be primary."

"Sounds like you're telling yourself that."

Her smile was wobbly. "I am. I'm selfish, I want my Family around me. But I truly do want my brother and sister to do what is right for *them*, a priority for *them*. Like we're leaving on this trip against my parents' wishes."

"And hiding the ultimate reason from my own Family. I get it. But I want them home." Words he kept repeating because they were true. He'd picked up the pace and now the ship, *Lady of Celta,* at pier twenty-six was in view.

"So you can try and fix your failure," Enata pressed.

So he was stubborn. "Maybe."

"Sometimes that can't be done. We can only live with the consequences of our actions."

"That's wisdom," said a voice in a noble accent.

They turned to a man nearly equal in height to Barton, somewhat older, who wore his long blond-brown hair in a tail. His hazel gaze was fixed on them.

Vinni T'Vine, the prophet of Celta. A surge of apprehension flowed from Barton to Enata, doubled to anxiety and poured back. Barton strove not to show that.

"Hey, Vinni," he said.

Vinni wore a puzzled expression. "I don't know exactly why I am here."

Barton felt Enata's pulse pound.

Vinni scrutinized them. "I . . . sense . . . that whatever you two will be doing, affects me somehow." His shoulders rolled uneasily.

"Enata and I are taking a wedding trip. A week, max. Do you see any problem with the voyage?" Barton asked as mildly as he could. Not many people were able to keep secrets from the prophet. But he'd known Vinni since they'd been boys and Barton kept his manner completely easy, acted as if he didn't lie with every thought and breath. Beside him, Enata showed nerves, but most people thought of her as high-strung, so that wouldn't tip Vinni off that she hid a secret from him.

Vinni's gaze had gone to the ship, beyond it and out to the ocean. "No-oo." He frowned. "A very odd trip . . ."

"We like odd," Enata said. "Will we be successful in, ah, bonding well?" She snuggled close to Barton, but he felt her aura, her unspoken questions, intensify. More like *Will we be successful in discovering what's happening with our loved ones?* Perhaps she thought that her intention might influence Vinni's gift, even if she phrased the question differently.

A long moment of silence with water lapping the stanchions came, then Vinni's expression lightened and he dipped his head. His eyes, always changeable when his Flair came upon him, returned to his standard hazel.

"Yes, you will be successful." Vinni's sharp gaze

pinned the both of them. "This is . . . whatever you are doing . . . something that is vital and must be done." He frowned at them, then his eyes widened and he raised his hands, stepped back and nearly shouted, "No, I don't want to know and I will *not* stay in your company to have you trigger more of my Flair!" The prophet vanished.

And Barton sensed the Captain of the ship behind him.

He turned. "Greetyou, Captain Mor."

The man grunted. "Come along, then. We best leave as soon as possible." He grimaced. "Wasn't supposed to return to Druida City so soon. But *she* said so, so here I am."

Enata curtsied. "Greetyou and thank you, Captain Mor."

He stared at her. "You'd be the Licorice Librarian."

"That's right."

"You're welcome." He turned and began clumping away. "You're welcome, too, Clover. Though I doubt you'll like the whole thing."

And ME!

The Captain stopped, whirled, stared at the small head poking out of Barton's duffle. "That's a kitten. I was told a FamCat. Perhaps."

I AM a CAT! Resup insisted.

Snorting, the Captain said, "You're a kitten." He snapped his fingers and a tiny orange floatation vest appeared in his hands. With gnarled but gentle fingers he put it on a frozen Resup. Enata had to use a spell to keep Barton's Fam quiet. He didn't like the vest, but understood why. Not only would the vest be easy to see, but it had a return-to-ship spell if Resup fell overboard.

* * *

It was the strangest sail . . . cruise Barton had ever experienced. He'd been out on a couple of FirstFamily noble's yachts, one dinner cruise off the coast as a Family celebration of a wedding anniversary, but never beyond the sight of land. And the *Lady of Celta*'s crew was far too minimal for a seagoing ship. Weirdest of all was the method of transportation. A septhour and a half out of Druida City, the Captain sailed into a strong current that simply pulled along the whole ship as if it was locked straight into that flow. That lasted for a good day and a half.

Near the beginning of the trip, Barton had felt ill, as if someone messed with his Familial bonds. As he sweated and held onto Enata's hand, he made her talk of Savi and Balansa . . . because their memories began to fade. Until the Captain told them the ship had reached the half way point to the island, where his cuzes were. Time away from their home and on the island? And distance? Barton figured those were factors in when such memories disappeared.

Though Enata questioned the Captain and got some answers which she noted down, the rest of the voyage Barton mostly watched Resup. Neither Captain nor crew paid much attention to him or the kitten.

The evening of the second day, they came into port in a wide bay surrounded by white cliffs. Only one dock thrust into the ocean.

≈ Chapter 17 ≈

They exited *Lady of Celta* by walking down a gangplank to a pier. Enata had her bag on an anti-grav follow spell, and Barton carried his duffle, Resup once again tucked inside and snoozing.

Though the surrounding scenery was stunning with high cliffs of pale rock with verdant green covering the top of them, one with a looming castle, her gaze went to the three people standing beyond the prow of the ship on the pier, two smaller ones in front of a tall man. A man with rusty hair the color of Glyssa's and eyes—though she couldn't see them—the color of her own. Reglis!

Her heart thumped hard in her chest.

Barton appeared more grim than intense and she wished she knew him well enough that she could drop a phrase into his mind to be easy on his young relatives.

Then he met her eyes and they warmed and a corner of his mouth lifted. *You do well enough in knowing me,* Barton sent to her mind.

The feeling is mutual, she said, then looked down the dock. Her eyes became accustomed to the dimness of the lowering sun dipping behind clouds and she ran toward the beloved, and now-well-recognized, shape of her brother Reglis, shouting his name.

At the same time, the thin young man, looking more like a boy than a legal adult, glanced up and jolted. She heard his gasp. He grabbed his younger sister and held her.

Then she reached Reglis and threw herself into

his arms. He smelled of honeysuckle.

"Enata! They told me to come to the pier, but I . . . " He choked and just grabbed her and they shook together. "I've missed you *so much.*"

"Me, too." She decided it wasn't the time to tell him of the vanishing memories of everyone, to interrogate him about the terrible, wrenching spell that someone laid on the Families of the Chosen.

Barton strode past them, sending a tender thought. *You talk to your brother.*

Thank you for giving me this time alone with him, she replied telepathically.

There is time enough, he ended, though his shoulders squared as he headed for his own lost ones.

Reglis said, "Tell me everything that's happened. About you," he glanced at Barton's very nice retreating butt, "and your very handsome and virile lover."

"My new husband."

"Congratulations!" Reglis squeezed her tight, and she recalled that he, too, had no HeartMate in this lifetime. "Tell me all, and about Glyssa and the parents."

"Glyssa is off with her HeartMate to the excavation of the starship *Lugh's Spear,* and will be one of the founders of a community there."

"What!" Reglis gasped. "They're excavating *Lugh's Spear?* How utterly fascinating! Tell me everything. Who's sponsoring—"

"The Elecampanes, of course, and Glyssa is the historian!"

"What a great opportunity. And she's found her

HeartMate?"

"An adventurer named Jace Bayrum?" Enata lifted her own brows, got a quick shake of his head.

"Never heard of him."

"All right . . ." And instead of talking about *The Chosen of Celta,* and all her questions, she began telling her brother all that had passed outside this island. She treasured the easy flow of emotion through their sibling link.

Barton wasn't quite sure to handle his own relatives, neither of them had run to *him.* But he did try to keep a nervous frown off his face, and stopped within the distance expected of Family.

"Greetyou, Savi." Barton gave the youngster a half bow, angled his body to Balansa and gave her the same. "Greetyou Balansa."

They didn't have any features that proclaimed them "Clover" to him, but then none of the Clovers had wildly original features. Something of a commonality of manner, maybe, but no special hawk nose or wide brow, or whatever, that marked them all.

As a matter of fact, Savi appeared downright handsome, for sure with finer features than Barton's own blunt ones. And Balansa would be a beauty. Good looking young ones.

"Barton," Savi said, belligerence in his voice.

Barton judged him to be an instant away from an argument, maybe even a swing of a fist that Barton had followed him and disrupted his current life, questioned his judgment.

"Let's take this down the dock," he said.

With a curl of his lips, Savi turned and marched

to solid ground, then stood that ground.

He spoke first. "I won't go back." His lips pressed together, he jutted his chin. "There is nothing there for me in Druida City, with the Clovers." He nearly spat the name. Expression seething with anger, he measured his gaze against Barton's. "You didn't care for us!" the cry of betrayal tore from his seventeen-year-old throat.

Barton stepped back, enough that he could bow low to the youngster. He also dropped his gaze, trusting in his reflexes to counter any strike from Savi. Keeping low, his sight on the ground, he said, "I admit my wrong. I admit the wrong of the Head of the Household in failing you and your sister, in the deficiency in the Clover Family elders in caring for you." He stayed that way for long moments, as he'd learned as a child younger than Balansa.

"I acknowledge your apologies," Savi said gruffly.

Straightening, Barton inclined his head. "But you don't accept them, as is your right."

"It shows a lack of graciousness," said the girl who hadn't spoken until now. Both Savi and Barton flinched. She sounded just like their mothers.

"I accept your apology. All your apologies," the young man said reluctantly. His lips firmed. "But I've made my choice and I'm not going back."

"You're sure? The Family will—"

A near ugly laugh. "The Family is already broken into high status and low status ranks. Walker, you and your lady," Savi jerked his head at Enata, "obviously another noblewomanthose who marry nobles or know nobles well—and those of us who don't."

That hadn't occurred to Barton, and it wasn't *quite* true. Yet. But now that he thought on it, he could see the stratification Savi accused them of. That must stop. Since the whole Family must work to make them all affluent nobles, within the Family they had to be fluid. Recognize potential, like the Flair this young man had, the beauty of this pair. Barton knew who to put in charge of this, Sedwy, the anthropologist, Walker's wife.

"If you want a noble marriage, we could arrange it," he said mildly.

"And if I'd come to you that winter when our parents died?"

"We would have drawn you into a Family to shelter and care for you," Barton said promptly. He looked at Balansa. "We will do so for you, now. And Savi, you know you qualify for your own home in Clover Compound."

"Not for me," Savi said. "The lady has explained my choices." He stood straight and tall, a powerfully Flaired young man whose potential the Clovers hadn't seen or appreciated. "She does not want unwilling colonists, reluctant *Chosen*." The last word, more like a title, rolled rich and full off Savi's tongue. "She has plans for me, and I intend to stay."

"The Lady? Of the Lady and Lord?" Barton probed.

Savi's face clouded. "It is not my place to say. But if you came to find out whether I am happy here, I am. I will stay." He spread his arm in a wide gesture encompassing the island. "The Chosen here are the Best of the Best."

"I hear you," Barton said.

Savi nodded to Barton, one adult to another, equal. "I am glad to see you, though, Barton. It's good."

A lot of words about the dance Savi had led him on lay on Barton's tongue. All too negative. He swallowed them. "I am glad you found your place, youn—," he stopped that word. "Savi." Turning to the man's sister, he asked, "What of you, Balansa? Has the lady spoken to you?"

Her face crumpled, and she brushed her hand against her brother's as if wanting him to take it. He didn't seem to feel the touch.

We're here! said Resup's teeny voice. He clawed at the tab of Barton's duffle, stuck his head out, sniffed lustily. *I smell you!* he caroled, gaze fixed on Savi. *You are sort of Clover.*

"A kitten Fam," Balansa cooed. She glanced up at Barton. "May I hold him?"

Since she'd mentally heard the Fam, too, she had good Flair. "Sure."

She plucked him from the duffle and held him against her chest. "You are beautiful!"

Of course, said Resup, *You smell like all Clover.*

"A kitten Fam," Savi repeated flatly. "And the Clover Family doesn't have many individuals with Fam companions."

"Neither does any other Family," Barton retorted.

"But those who do have Fams are of the inner circle, privileged Clovers."

All right, the boy remained angry. Let him beat that anger against Barton, he could take it. "Says the man who is *Chosen,*" Barton retorted. "*Chosen* above all other Clovers." Because he had been angry with his lot? Other Clovers weren't, so whoever . . .

"That's right." Savi's voice, and his face, became rapt. He angled a little, his stare fixed, and Barton turned to look . . . at the sun, caught in the last bank of clouds before it set, shooting rays of yellow and pink up into the sky and coating the water below with a stream of the same colors. The rest of the world took on a bluish tinge of oncoming night. With a jolt, Barton understood that Savi was just appreciating this simple pleasure. Taking time from his day to watch the sun set because it was beautiful.

After a moment, Savi sighed, glanced back to Barton and said, equally easily, "I'm happy here, Barton. I'm happy with my choices. I have a good life, and a girlfriend." His smile came sudden and blinding. "And I will ask the lady for a Fam. She'll arrange one." He put his hand on his sister's back. "Shall we return to the Castle?"

Slowly Balansa held Resup out to Barton.

"I think we're all going to the same place." He looked over to Enata and Reglis who strolled toward them, heads still bent in conversation. "We'll catch up with you. Keep Resup until then, if he wants to go with you."

I have never been in a Castle! I would like to see one. I would like to run. Barton does not run enough.

Balansa grinned. "Thanks!"

"I can't promise a Fam kitten or cat," Barton said, observing Savi from the corner of his eyes, "but I bet I could get you a FamFox kit, Balansa. We have that fox den outside the Compound."

Joy filled her eyes. And Savi said nothing. Didn't

insist that his sister stay. Interesting.

Savi and Balansa took off, Savi at a lope and Balansa at a run, on the criss-crossing path up the hill.

When Enata and her brother caught up to Barton, she put her arm around his waist, making them a unit. "Reglis, this is my husband, Barton Clover. Barton, this is my brother, Reglis Licorice." She nearly sang the last phrase.

≈ Chapter 18 ≈

Putting his hands around her face, Reglis kissed her forehead. "I am so glad you found a husband dear to your heart." Reglis pivoted and kissed Barton on the cheek. "I'm glad you found my sister." Reglis stepped back. "Neither Enata nor I have HeartMates for this lifetime, but we both longed for a husband and partner. You look to be well-matched."

"By Saille T'Willow himself," Barton said dryly. He waited a beat. "As you would be if you returned to Druida City."

Reglis shook his head. "My life is here. I have a vocation I cannot abandon. We'll talk later about that and why you're here. Tomorrow, perhaps. Now I'll leave you to proceed to Celta's Castle at your own pace while watching the sun set. I do have duties. You will be welcome at the castle and please consider it your home for as long as you are here."

After another smile and nod to them, he teleported away.

Barton took Enata's hand and they began to walk up the only visible path.

"So how much did you learn about this mysterious lady?"

"Lady?"

"That's what Savi called her."

"Not enough," Enata said.

He looked at her, noted the worry line twisted between her brows, and squeezed her fingers. "Both Savi and Reglis had a point."

"What?"

"We should enjoy the sunset." Barton paused as she turned and sighed at the brilliant colors painting sky and sea. "And be glad of steady land under our feet, a good dinner, and loving in a bed."

"You're right."

By the time they reached the huge double wooden doors of Celta's Castle, the walk, the evening and the warmth and humidity of the atmosphere had worked on Enata so that serenity pervaded her.

Whatever else, she had found her brother, and renewed her bond with him. That part of her trauma had disappeared.

The castle itself consisted of tall walls, both round and square towers, all of a reddish stone and set on a cliff overlooking the bay.

* * *

Barton awoke in the best bed he'd ever slept in the next morning. A nearly blasphemous thought for a man from the Clover Fine Furniture Family. He also woke up with, of course, the best woman he'd ever had curled next to him. High windows at the top of the walls opened to island air, wafting in humid breezes ladened with the scent of lush tropical flowers.

Really, the only irritating item was that he woke up because his FamKitten was hopping on him, claws not quite sheathed.

Barton grunted.

Good morning, FamMan Barton! the little cat trilled-purred.

"Uhn," said Enata, raising her lashes a little.

Good morning, FamWoman Enata! I NEED FOOD, then we need to explore the island!

Enata shuddered against Barton. He began to suspect she wasn't a morning person. That, maybe, she was even a *night* person. She sure had been lively the night before when they'd entered this beautiful room and she'd seen the magnificent carved four poster bed. He'd appreciated her energy, then.

Hop. Hop. Hop. A little tongue swiping across his cheek.

I ate all the furrabeast bites you had for the trip! I can't open the no-time! I'm HUNNGGRY!

Barton slipped from the bed. Resup sailed from the bedsponge to land in front of him, twitching a tiny tail.

I will sit on your foot and ride as you go to the sitting room and get Me food! He matched his words with action, plopping himself on Barton's foot.

"Watch the claws, cat. And what about the vibrations?" Barton asked.

Your vibrations match the ground now, Resup said.

"Huh." Each step careful, Barton walked to the sitting room. Sure enough, his duffle lay half off the seat the chair where he'd dropped it, gaping open, clothes and other stuff spilling out. Not one tiny shred of furrabeast bites, or jerky, or even clucker kibble remained. Spying a cabinet that looked a lot like the no-time food storage units at home, he ran his fingers along the top.

Weird, alien energy. Not really Flair-type energy, or Flair-tech, like he'd lived with all of his life. This no-time wasn't powered by the same stuff he was used to. But he opened it and found a pouch of tiny clucker cubes, ripped it and dumped them on a plate that had been stowed atop the no-time.

Absently listening to Resup munch, Barton expanded his senses. The same kind of energy hummed throughout the castle, only slightly augmented by Flair. Striding toward a window embrasure, he thinned the shield to nothing and drew in a breath to the bottom of his lungs. Plenty of energy and power, some of it Flair, most not.

Something to consider.

Then Enata came up behind him and put her arms around him and he figured it was time to return to bed. Their appointment with Reglis wasn't for a good septhour and a half.

* * *

Barton leaned against a paneled wall on the second floor of one of the round towers. The chamber encompassed the whole floor, with windows that could be thinned from stone to clear, or even to nothing by Flair. This room full of books, papyrus, vizes and recording spheres was Reglis Licorice's personal library.

The man had done well for himself.

Barton wanted to pace, *had* given the room a good pace or two as he studied the windows in between the bookcases. He'd looked out every one, checking the view. To the east and below he could easily see the bay and, in the opposite direction, what he believed to be the far edge of the island, maybe even a tinier island in the ocean beyond. In the middle of the land mass sat a gigantic, blue sapphire jewel of a lake . . . It appeared as though the island had been formed around the lake. He wondered if it was fresh or salt water. With the oddness of this whole place, it was probably fresh.

Enata had scrutinized the books and other stuff before sitting down in a large club chair to calmly await her brother. Like Barton, she wore professional garb. Hers was a long tunic split up the sides from below her knees to the top of her thighs, with trous beneath. Her tunic had rectangular sleeved pockets. He wore just-broken-in leathers, suitable for outside. He fully intended to take some island paths after the meeting, keep the exploration of Celta's Castle for later, though Resup had other ideas. He'd thrown a kitten tantrum when Barton suggested he accompany them to meet Enata's brother. Resup preferred to nose around the building. Barton had only wanted the kitten to stay inside, so they both won.

Barton and Enata had been early for the meeting. Since Reglis should show up in two minutes, Barton had stopped his circumnavigation of the room.

The door opened and Enata flew to the door to hug and be hugged by her brother.

Barton sensed the emotional flow between the siblings, glad his lady had that bond back. She held on tight until her brother began to appear uncomfortable and raised his brows at Barton. So he trod over and put his hand on her shoulder. "Come on, dear one, give Reglis time to answer our questions."

She nodded, then snuffled, and wiped the dampness of her eyes on his Flaired shirt, an intimacy that pleased him. Draping an arm around her shoulders, he led her to a wing back chair, and urged her to sit. He stood next to her, trying to look casual, but the moment had come and he thrummed with questions.

Reglis took a chair close to her, and Barton speared him with a gaze. "So who summoned us here?"

Head tilted, a touch of amusement on his lips and a dare in his eyes, Reglis said, "Can't you guess?"

"No," Barton replied flatly.

"Think big."

Barton shrugged. He sensed Enata's mind zipping through ideas.

"All right, think *huge,*" Reglis spread his arms wide.

"Reg-lis!" Enata protested.

He leaned back in his chair and his face became serious. "Usually by the time we arrive here, we've been prepared. Perhaps that didn't occur with you. But I can't tell you. You must guess. It's the rule," he paused. "That is, I can't tell you at all, Barton. Eventually, I believe, Enata will be . . . ah . . . contacted."

Displaying weakness or not, Barton got up and paced. "I think better on my feet."

"Of course," Reglis said easily. Still felt like a weakness to Barton. After a couple of circuits of the room he stopped at the east window and looked out at the bay, beyond those cliffs at the ocean separating the island and Druida City. Slowly, he began to winnow every hint he'd heard, put the puzzle together.

She. *The Lady of Celta*. The name of the sailing ship between this lost island and the peninsula holding Druida City.

An island not shown on any maps.

Not shown when the Earthan ships circling the planet recorded its geography as they landed. A shrouded island, even then?

Or maybe a new island, but how could that be?

An island especially formed for the Chosen of Celta.

By the Lady of Celta.

But not the goddess his culture worshipped, the partner to the Lord, the Celtic Lady and Lord that they, humans from Earth, had brought with them to form the basis of a new society on this planet.

Huge.

Vibrations in the ground, "bad" and not compatible to the Fam animals in Druida City, but "the same" as the ground here.

He'd sensed alien magic, not human psi-Flair or Flair technology all around.

But they were not the natives. *They* were the aliens.

And part of the culture they'd developed was that every particle of the universe was alive. Rocks. Mountains. Stars.

A planet.

Celta's Castle. Celta's Chosen.

An entity who could erase a person from the mind of everyone who'd ever known or known of that person.

He thought his mind exploded, snatched at the far reaches of it, the most incredible thought. He must be wrong. He'd sound foolish if he said what he was thinking. But he coughed, turned to look at Reglis and Enata. "The planet. This planet has—is—alive. Is a being, an entity. Celta."

≈ Chapter 19 ≈

Reglis grinned and clapped once. "Well done, Barton! I never would have guessed. Never allowed my mind to extrapolate such a notion." He glanced at his sister. "How about you, Enata?"

Enata looked flabbergasted, her eyes unfocused, her lips parted. She shook her head, struggling to overcome disbelief, Barton thought.

He rolled his shoulders. So he'd pulled a guess from the farthest, most fantastic edges of his mind and it had been right, still fliggering staggering, but right. He stared at Reglis, who appeared pleased.

"So we've discovered the *who,*" Barton grated the words out. "We can get to *why* later."

"Why is very important," both Licorices said at the same time, Enata's voice squeaky high.

"No. What's very important is the ill effects this is having on everyone." Barton's gaze bore into Reglis'. The man blinked. "You serve this lady?"

"The lady avatar of the planet Celta? Yes, I do." He spread his arms wide. "Ill effects? I am fine. The Chosen are fine." He glanced away. "The lady has learned how to deal with human minds." Barton got the impression that the lady had learned by trial and error, like by breaking fragile human minds.

"Not well enough," Barton said. "Enata's been sick since the beginning of the month, when the lady began messing with her head."

"What!"

Barton scooped Enata out of her chair, sat himself, and kept her on his lap. Knowing his face tightened, he kept his voice smooth and quiet. "Do you realize what that . . . what Celta has been doing to your sister? All this month she's been going to that vault of yours to see a new book, *The Chosen of Celta.*" He jutted his chin to a big floating book in the corner. It looked larger than the one he'd seen in the vault. His hands soothed Enata. She rested against him.

Grit entered Barton's tones. "And every time Enata left, that thing—" He stopped and coughed. "—the great entity who is our home," he said aloud to remind himself he did love the planet, not to mention it could probably crush him with a thought. "That is to say, Celta removed her memories. So she's been bouncing back and forth between remembering you and not. Tore her up emotionally. There have also been physical side effects."

Reglis stared at them, face paling. "No," he whispered. "I didn't know."

"Celta has been hard on Enata." He pinned the shocked man with his most intimidating gaze. "I want a Healer called to check her out. You *do* have Healers, don't you?"

"Of course." Reglis drew himself up.

"Look at her." Barton swept a hand along his beloved. Hardened his heart. "Does she match your memory? She's too thin and pale."

"I'm better now," she murmured.

Reglis scowled.

"Speaking of memories. Celta doesn't tell you she wipes you from the memories of all who knew you, even knew *of* you, does she? She doesn't inform you of that when she calls you and tells you that you're Chosen, or once you're here."

Pure shock rolled over Reglis' face, trembled down his body. He reached for a chair, groped his way into it.

"I see you can figure out the ramifications of that—broken minds, fractures in a Family missing one of their members and not knowing that, inexplicable psychological problems, behavioral problems."

Enata said, "I was mean, really mean to Glyssa, and not just personally, but professionally, in a professional setting." She rubbed her forehead, then she dropped her hand. "The Hazels . . . I don't think they've been quite right for a long time. Functioning, but not *right*. You have a Calluna Heather Hazel here. Is she a Healer?"

A white-faced Reglis nodded. "Yes, but not at Celta's Castle. I'll call our Healer. He's very good, especially with the mind . . . he helps us adjust."

"You obviously remember your Families," Barton said.

"Yes, of course. We are given the choice to live here or not, accept the vocation offered or not."

"I'm thinking those who don't take Celta up on the offer don't remember the fact. Choice is a step in the right direction. Celta probably realized that rebellious humans don't fit her needs," Barton muttered.

Enata asked softly, "How do you feel knowing that we have no memory of you?"

Now Reglis looked just plain sick. "I'm calling the Healer. He's a native." His head tilted as if he spoke telepathically.

"The Healer was born and raised here?" Barton asked.

"Yes." Reglis popped from his chair. "He'll be along shortly. He's working with Captain Mor and the crew. The voyages are hard on them."

"Maybe because of the memory thing," Barton said. "Maybe it comes and goes with them."

Reglis' mouth flattened. "I've asked Corylus Hazel and Calluna Heather Hazel, the *Chosen* before me, to come, too."

"Good, get this entire mess all thrashed out," Barton said. "You can tell us more of Celta while we wait."

The sizzle of his anger cycling through their link made Enata nervy, along with his tense muscles. She shifted in his lap, caught a motion from the corner of her eye. "What's that volume floating in the corner?"

Reglis raised his hand and the book, twice as large as the one in Security Vault One in the PublicLibrary, floated over to them.

"This is the complete and unabridged record of Celta's Chosen."

She rose to her feet, stalked over to the book, felt some of Barton's anger fade to her own irritation and his curiosity match hers. "The PublicLibrary has an *abridged* version!"

A familiar smile wisped across Reglis' lips. "I know how annoying that is for you." His eyes narrowed and he tilted his head. "*Perhaps* we can provide a copy." He tapped the opened page with a forefinger and Enata saw his small, precise writing.

"Your notes," she breathed. "And everyone else's?"

Reglis nodded. "Perhaps I can convince Celta to duplicate this in Security Vault One."

"How?" Barton asked. "How does this all work?"

"Magic." Reglis rolled a shoulder. "Celta is a strong planet, not weak like the crippled Earth our forebears left. Intelligent and skilled. Magic, psi power, Flair, call it what you will, but we are puny compared to her."

"Her?" questioned Barton.

"Like our Residences, and the starship *Nuada's Sword*, the planet chose a sex to interact with us better." A quick smile. "I think because the first librarian she picked was male and preferred women. He listened to her telepathic conversation."

"A powerful planetary being? Anyone would."

Reglis' brows went up. "You'd be surprised what some people prefer to ignore."

"I never ignore voices in my head," Barton said, joining her to look at the book. "Unless they're nagging Family."

They all laughed.

"So," Reglis prompted. "Questions?"

"Why us?" Barton flicked a hand toward Reglis, then Enata and himself.

"I—" Reglis stopped and tilted his head for a long moment, nodded, then met Enata's gaze, looked at Barton. "I was going to tell you my own deductions, but now I will be speaking for the planet, Celta, as we call her. Naturally, she did not think of herself as that until our ancestors, the colonists from Earth, arrived."

"What did she—" Enata began.

Barton's hand dropped to her shoulder again.

"You librarians get distracted. Keep on topic. Why us? Why the other's she's taken in . . . our lifetimes?" He paused. "Specifically."

"Specifically," Reglis repeated, an odd note in his voice, then, "Ouch!" A pause. "You're forgiven. Do not forget you can burn out our minds while talking to us."

Enata gasped, Barton went stiff beside her.

Reglis flinched and grimaced, then said, "Yes, all mended. Thank you." He turned his head back toward them. "Celta prefers to have a PublicLibrarian in Druida City as a failsafe, should something happen to the general populace of our planet, the librarian would know to bring the survivors here." Reglis cleared his throat. "We are a delicate species to her, and there is only so much changing to herself she is willing to do so we might adapt."

"All . . . right," Barton said. "So that's Enata. Why me?"

"For the same reason she chose Savi. Because you are Clovers, the most prolific Family of us all."

Enata heard him grinding his teeth. "Oh. So she's not giving up Savi?"

"No, but Balansa can leave." Reglis touched his temple, then his head dropped. Without looking at them, he said, "She confirms that she's tampered with memories. And states that when you leave, you will lose your memories of here."

≈ Chapter 20 ≈

At that moment a knock came on the door and the doctor strode in. A brusque individual called Heathrun, he examined Enata, then gave her some Healing energy that made her feel better than she had in a long time.

But he'd riled Reglis. Apparently Heathrun knew of the memory loss, and as a native, knew more than Reglis in general. They began to argue about how to deal with Celta and the planet's habit of erasing memories.

Barton grabbed her and excused them both for lunch. Neither of the men paid attention to them leaving.

They descended the tower staircase and walked through the big building to the large front entrance hall. Not a lot of people populated the castle, and they all wore simple trous and embroidered shirts, made of excellent fabric.

"I want to get out of here, you game?" asked Barton.

"Absolutely."

He glanced down at her, and tension left his face. "You're feeling fine?"

Smiling up at him, she said, "Oh, yes. Heathrun helped a lot. I feel completely on balance." She let a gleam come into her eyes. "Though later we might want to practice that very healthful sex he mentioned."

"Sounds good to me. You need to change clothes for a tramp around the island?"

She whisked a hand down her outfit. "There, I've

activated the spell for outside. It should handle tramping."

"Good. I'll call Resup."

Enata waited at the double front doors as Barton lifted his chin and called, aloud and with his mind, *Teleport to me! We're heading out of the castle.*

Whee! I am here! I have been ALL OVER the castle. People love Me, of course. Resup landed on all four paws in front of them. Stuff sticking to his whiskers looked suspiciously like sweet white mousse.

Barton put the cat on his padded shoulder and they walked up to the doors, which opened for them.

"Celta's Castle must be on the way to becoming a Residence," Enata said.

They stepped into sunshine that spilled brilliant light around them. The air smelled of verdant plantlife and crisp ocean. Below she could see the bay and the ship that had brought them.

And then two people rose from a bench set in one side of the garden flanking the entrance, and hesitantly walked up the gravel path to them. Savi and Balansa.

Savi made a jerky bow, Balansa a smoother curtsey.

"We're inviting you to lunch in the village." Savi's chin lifted with pride. "I will show you my house, and introduce you to my girlfriend. We also need to talk to you about . . . things."

Barton bowed. "I am always at your service."

Balansa's expression pinched. Enata didn't know if Barton noticed that or not.

The village was very picturesque, with an odd

mixture of architectural styles. Enata studied it, knowing she'd seen images of a village like this before. Then she realized it was modeled after Portmeirion on Earth.

Savi showed off his small whitewashed cottage and lovely garden, justly proud of it. He preferred to live in the village in a separate cottage. Not at all like the linked houses of Clover Compound. They met his equally lovely native girlfriend at a clothing workshop.

Lunch at an outside cafe provided excellent food with flavors new but tasty to Enata. They all concentrated on their food, including Resup who charmed everyone he met, including the kitchen staff. He fell asleep before the waiter swept away the dishes.

Savi shifted in his seat, then stated, "Balansa isn't as happy here as I am."

Gently, Barton said, "You must know that both of you can come back with me and Enata. We are your Family, and will always welcome you."

"I'm staying," Savi stated.

Balansa pleated the cloth softleaf on her lap. "I don't know what to do."

Savi sat straight. "If Balansa returns, will you promise to place her in a good Clover Family unit, and ensure she's tested for Flair and is given the choice of a good career? Make certain she finds a good husband?"

"I promise," Barton said immediately. "I'm strongly recommending that those you call the most privileged Clovers don't all live in the original and oldest block of Clover Compound. Walker himself resides in the newer southern block. We'll be spreading out. I promise I will treat Balansa as if she was my sister."

For a moment Savi stared at Barton, then switched his gaze to Enata. "I will take your word on that." He looked at his sister, reached both hands across the table and held them out until she took them. "I love you, Balansa. You are my sister and can always stay with me."

"I love you, too," Balansa said.

"You can always come back here, I promise."

Balansa bobbed her head.

But Enata found her eyes meeting Barton's. Neither of them expected that the lady of Celta would let Balansa keep her memories of her only immediate Family member.

Enata's throat closed so she couldn't say one word after that.

Savi and Balansa walked back up to Celta's Castle with Barton and Enata, but they went their separate ways in the great hall. Barton watched Balansa trudge toward the storerooms where she'd inventory foodstuffs.

"Cyfrinach Island is pretty," Enata said. "Tropical. I've never been to anywhere tropical, and I'd like to walk around a little."

"It's nice," Barton agreed, putting his arm around her waist. "How long do you want to stay? I'd just as soon go home when our questions are answered and our business is done. A quick break would be better for Balansa, too."

Enata sighed. "You're right. Not a true wedding trip is this. I do want to see more of the island instead of Reglis' library."

Barton chuckled. "I'd never thought I'd hear that."

"Well, you did. And now it's time to meet with Reglis again."

Resup perked up from his seat on Barton's shoulder. *I will go with you. I have not been to this interesting library.*

When they entered the room, Resup wandered the chamber, poking his nose into the lower bookcases and jumping on window seats while Enata took her chair, and Barton hitched a hip on the arm of that chair.

This time Reglis paced, under the guise of keeping an eye on the kitten.

Still aching from lunch with Savi and Balansa, Barton began the pressure. "By now you know of the compulsion laid on Enata and my obsession."

Reglis pinched the skin between his brows. "I reviewed *The Chosen of Celta* and that seems to be standard procedure for those Celta wishes to visit Cyfrinach Island."

"To visit, not to stay," Barton kept his voice flat.

"That's right. I, myself, had vivid dreams, as do most who are Chosen. As for compulsions and obsessions, those are . . . ah . . . methods Celta uses to judge people."

Enata straightened. "I'm tired of being judged, of having to prove myself. Proving myself to Celta, to the Clovers, to the matchmaker T'Willow, even."

"You never did like being tested, manipulated," Reglis murmured.

"No, I didn't." She folded her arms and glared at

her brother. "I trust, that since we are here, we passed Celta's tests."

Nodding, Reglis said, "That's right."

No one tested Me. I am special, Resup said, kneading a window seat. *I will watch the ship, now.*

He curled up and slept.

Reglis' smile at the Fam was brief, then his gaze met Barton's with melancholy intensity. "You, sis, will remember. The PublicLibrarians of Druida do." He cleared his throat. "I've heard that Balansa Clover might return with you to Druida City. Neither Balansa nor Barton will remember anything."

"Your Celta is very hard on those left behind when the Chosen leave!" Her breasts rose as she inhaled. "I suppose you were chosen because you are the current librarian here?"

"Yes, the archivist."

"What of the others Chosen?" Barton asked.

A knock came at the door and Reglis' shoulders sank with relief. "Enter," he called.

A couple dressed in the standard work clothes but of fine material came in, hand in hand. They looked in their early thirties. "You requested we come to Celta's Castle, Master Librarian?"

"That's right, Corylus." Reglis smiled, gesturing for the couple to take the twoseat perpendicular to his and Barton's chair. Enata's face smoothed in professional welcome.

Gut still tight with anger, Barton reached out and grasped her wrist, tugged. He wanted her close. Maybe he couldn't defend her from a planetary being, but he could try to keep her safe with everything in him.

This time Enata stood with hands inside her opposite sleeves.

≈ Chapter 21 ≈

Barton narrowed his eyes. "Surely you're a Hazel," he said to the man.

The guy nodded. "Corylus Hazel."

"Another FirstChild? Born before Coll Hazel and Avellana?" Barton pressed.

"That's right. How is my Family doing?"

"Well," Barton said, before Enata could explain in detail. They only wanted basic reassurance. They had chosen to turn their backs on their Families and come to this island and begin a new life. Chosen to stay.

"I study the ocean like my father, Chess Rowan T'Hazel," the guy said.

"And I am Calluna Heather Hazel, a Healer," the woman said, "The primary Healer in the town of Newdru."

Studying her, Barton asked, "You're also a member of the FirstFamilies, the Heathers?"

She nodded, kept her arm linked in her husband's. Probably HeartMates. Which, like the high status—the Rowans, the Hazels, the Heathers were all Families with the greatest Flair—probably explained why the planet Chose them to be its own private stock of humans. Because that's what this all came down to. The planet called the best to this island to keep them safe from the misfortunes that might afflict the people on the continents.

And, no doubt, to breed them. Did they mind being in a breeding program?

He caught Enata's eye. She'd sense the anger simmering through him, ready to spark, to roar. To destroy the other couple's complacency. She shook her head.

"Your Families are doing very well," Enata affirmed.

"Even Avellana?" Corylus asked. "She was brain damaged at three." His forehead lined.

"She's survived the dreamquests to free her Flair, her Passages," Enata said.

"Good!"

The woman squeezed her HeartMate's hand. "I told you it would be all right."

"Yes."

Corylus stared at them. "Are you new residents here?"

"No," Barton said.

"My sister, Enata Licorice, will be the mainland PublicLibrarian who knows of us."

"Oh, good."

"I wanted to meet you," Enata said smoothly, standing as her brother had. "Those whom I might have known or met before."

The Hazel-Heather pairing rose, too. The woman smiled impishly. "We haven't been kidnapped, and are very happy with our lives." She paused. "And our four children." The last was said with pride. It was rare for FirstFamily nobles to have more than one or two children, especially if they married within their rank.

"Thank you for speaking with us," Enata said.

"It's fun to come to Celta's Castle now and again," Calluna said.

"Feel free to stay for dinner and overnight," Reglis offered.

"Sure." Corylus Hazel chuckled. "Good to be without the children for a night." He waved to Barton and Enata. "Later."

"Later," Barton said, and closed the door behind them.

"Anything else?" asked Reglis.

"Of course," Enata said. "Why were they Chosen?"

Barton grunted and Enata and Reglis looked at him. "I'm thinking it was him, Corylus Hazel, and they were HeartMates so Calluna came along. It must be because of Avellana. She's very different, and she's a full sibling to Corylus. Has to do with whatever happened when Avellana was seven . . ." There were hushed rumors something *major* had happened, but Barton didn't know what, though he thought his brother Walker did and kept the secret . . . "the Hazels were chosen *before* the event. Which means Celta knew what was coming up . . . somehow. Maybe. Probably."

"We cannot comprehend the depths of her intelligence," Reglis said, sitting on the window seat next to Resup and stroking the cat, who stretched out under his hand.

"I imagine not." Time to work around to saying out loud what he thought what else this was all about. "Just before we embarked, we spoke with Vinni T'Vine."

Reglis shook his head, smiling. "Vinni T'Vine, the prophet. What did he see for you?"

"It was about this trip. He's HeartMate to Avellana Hazel, so he's been affected by this, too. Do you have any recent Vines, as well?"

"No Vines lately," Reglis said. "Of course Celta is very interested in him and his Family and the prophecies." Reglis shifted. "But a couple of Vines were included at the start of her, ah, sequestration program."

Barton stared at him. "She, the planet, is breeding you all. And she's breeding a line of Vines, prophets?"

Reglis reddened. "We have communities here. Of course we fall in love and marry. Of course there are also HeartMate bonds, which, as I understand it, is *not* a phenomena instituted by her. HeartMates and HeartBonding is in our Earthan genetic material."

"That's really interesting," Barton said.

"Yes." Reglis nodded.

"But Celta is *choosing* you for certain characteristics. Culling, say, the best of the best, and breeding you to be better suited to the environment. That doesn't disturb you?"

"No more than the fact that the FirstFamilies themselves have been breeding for psi power since before the generational starships landed," Reglis snapped. "Or look at you Clovers. Now ennobled from Commoners. Don't tell me that you don't want to encourage stronger Flair in your youngsters. That you aren't drawing nobles into your Family to marry." He stared pointedly at Enata.

She jumped to her feet. "Barton and I were matched by GreatLord Saille T'Willow. As you could be if you came home with us." She swallowed. "I wouldn't have cared if he was a Commoner, nor would he have cared had I been one."

Reglis' gaze softened. He came over, lifted her hand and kissed it. "I understand."

Enata closed her eyes. "The feel of the natural cycling of Family energy between us is good." She sighed out audibly. "I've missed you so much. We were so close, then you weren't even in my recollection. Glyssa had her deep friendships with Camellia Darjeeling and Tiana Mugwort, so that must have helped her. . . and she's met her HeartMate." Enata's lips trembled. "I'm glad I won't be forgetting you again."

"Me, too. But I'm not going back to Druida City." He stood tall. "Since Celta began bringing people here, there's always been a Licorice Librarian. And a Licorice Librarian in Druida City as a failsafe."

"How nice for you, Enata and Reglis." Barton sucked in a breath. "I mean that. It's good that Enata won't be remembering and forgetting and remembering and her health crashing. But let me get this straight. I—and all my Family—will forget Savi."

"That's right." Reglis' stance became defensive. Didn't matter, Barton could take the guy easily. He wondered if Celta had any fighters here, then dismissed the thought. He was in no mood to think well of the planet, to appease the being. "But you will remember us. You all remember your Families and friends."

"Yes."

"And Celta lets you think that your friends and Families remember you."

Reglis dropped his eyes. "I didn't know about this before. We'll talk to her."

"Good luck with that." Barton offered his elbow

to Enata. "We'd like to breathe some more tropical air."

She smiled at her brother, then took Barton's arm. "That sounds good."

With a snap of his fingers, Barton translocated Resup to his shoulder.

Out to explore, brother of FamWoman. Fun! I will show everyone else how wonderful FAMS are! See you later.

Reglis cleared his throat. "Celta also indicated that she may provide you with a mobile Healer, Enata, since she will be contacting you."

"A mobile Healer? What does that mean?"

Shrugging, Reglis said, "I don't know, but she seemed impressed with Resup."

Of course, said the kitten.

"Do you have any idea when Celta will contact me?" Enata asked.

Reglis blew out a breath. "In her own time."

"Which, being a planet, might be, oh, a century or so?" Barton said. "We don't have that kind of time. As far as everyone believes, we're on our wedding trip. One week from today, we need to be back home."

"If she wants me to be the fail-safe person, the Celtan Librarian embedded in human culture, she must move quickly," Enata added. She withdrew her hand from Barton's arm to momentarily hug her brother, and then they left the library.

As far as Barton was concerned, he didn't care if he ever saw that room again. He brooded as Enata and Resup chattered on their way back to their quarters, Enata to change clothes for a walk atop the long ridge behind Celta's Castle.

Celta's Castle. Celta's Chosen.

Of whom Savi was one, but not Balansa. Or Barton.

He didn't know how she might think of humans . . . less than a regular person did the shortest-lived pet, probably. Interesting to watch and mold. And breed.

Barton was damn sure that the being of Celta herself wasn't entirely beneficent. No doubt in his mind that when she'd first tried to make contact with the frail and delicate humans, she'd driven them mad or killed them. She must have left a trail of bodies behind her on this quest of hers.

He was determined that Enata, Savi, and Balansa would not be such victims.

≈ Chapter 22 ≈

The next morning, they awoke naturally with the sunlight coming through their windows, had a leisurely breakfast in their rooms and played with the kitten.

Barton had been tagged by the head of the island's guard force—a native—to talk about security matters and running a Family like the chosen on the island. The woman Guarda Chief had figured Clover Compound would be comparable to the island and its population.

So Enata took her first solitary walk around the island. Not precisely *around,* but atop another ridge angled inland, then dropping down a path in the direction of the big lake that she hoped she might see in person.

The thick forest of the island resounded with birdsong and the movement of animals, a gorgeous melody. Celta taking care of her special creatures.

Of which Enata's brother was one. That both pleased and hurt. It would truly rip at her when she left. Lady and Lord, she prayed Reglis was right and she would not lose her memory again. She'd figure out how to bargain with the planet if she needed to make that happen.

A tuneful warbling lilted into her mind. *I have a beautiful tail, look at my beautiful tail. I have a beautiful wings, how wondrous is the color of shading on my beautiful wings. I am happy I am beautiful. I am happy I am alive. I am happy I can SING!*

The complete good cheer of the bird stopped

Enata, had her rerunning her thoughts, flipping them to positive instead of negative. Concentrate on the positive.

She had a fabulous husband, one who loved her and whom she loved. A man she'd build a life with and who would help her heal any wounds given to her by this whole mess—wait, that was negative again.

Take it down to absolute simplicity.

The sun on her face, the scent of luxuriant forest and hint of sea, the colorful flowers around her, gave her pleasure. She felt good and glad to be alive.

She loved her husband and he loved her. Wondrous.

She enjoyed being with her brother again, and this unique experience intrigued her.

The sex with Barton was fantastic.

Yes, now she smiled.

Chirp. Chirp. Chirp. The bowing of a branchlet attracted her and she looked up, stunned at the beauty of the bird. The front of its head, above its beak to the backs of its eyes showed a deep pink, with a slash of yellow curving over amber eyes. The rest of its head was a pale gray. It had a bib of short gray-green feathers, then color again below that—yellow shading to rich orange, pink in the center, orange and yellow. The bird lifted her deep green wings and flicked the same color tail.

Hello, woman.

Hello, beautiful bird!

I AM beautiful. You are very beautiful, too. I like your hair.

It certainly waved more here than back in Druida

City, especially since she didn't confine it but wore it down, and her hair began lightening again.

The lady wound her song with mine and told me that I am to be a companion with you. Does that please you? It pleases me!

Enata answered, *Yes! It does please me! Many people back where I come from have a special bond with a feathered or furred companion.*

The bird flew to her shoulder, plucked at Enata's hair with her beak as if considering the thickness and consistency. *I DO like your hair.*

Enata raised a hand and brushed the back of it over the short green-gray feathers of the bird's side. *I like your feathers.*

Soft! they both said together. Enata smiled and the bird clicked her beak as if in satisfaction.

Chirping, then nuzzling her head against Enata's chin, the bird whispered into her mind, *The lady said I would like the patterns of your thoughts, and I do!*

Enata choked, but replied mentally, *Thank you. I like the song of your thoughts, too.*

A tiny peck. *I am to make sure the rhythm of your thoughts always stays beautiful.*

"A mobile Healer," Enata murmured.

I am called rose crowned fruit dove, the bird lilted. *But many are called that.* She looked expectantly at Enata. *So I get a PERSONAL name from you.*

With the lightest touch, Enata said aloud, "I will call you, Glabra."

It has nice sounds. Thank you.

"Let's walk back to the castle. We can bond during this lovely morning. And I want to introduce you to my mate and *his* Fam."

Glabra warbled in pleasure.

That Enata had found a Fam pleased Barton and he bowed to her and welcomed her into the Clover Family. The situation did *not* please Resup who hissed, and pouted, and only came around to acceptance after Barton had let the kitten sit on his head again.

* * *

After lunch, restlessness pervaded Enata. "I can't sit still," she grumbled when they inspected the herb gardens. Glabra sang her joy at bathing in a fountain as Resup watched with disdain.

Tilting his head, Barton stopped in front of her and took both her hands. His knees dipped a little in what he called sinking into his balance. Enata had barely recalled that from her grovestudy self-defense days. More fighting training lay ahead of her. Not something she'd ever contemplated.

He closed his eyes and she understood that he checked their bond, then his lips thinned as his eyelids opened. "I understand that feeling. Obsession."

"Oh. So Celta is calling me."

"Sounds right."

She drew a hand away from his, lifted it, "Come along, Glabra, we go to hear the lady." Enata's voice sounded a little ragged to herself.

Glabra flew, but Resup teleported to Barton's shoulder in a showy move.

Ah! Glabra sang. *We go to the glade in the grove, the glade in the grove for the lady!*

"You can show us," Enata said.

Yes, follow me!

I will show you a lot of Druida City, Resup said.

Barton snorted, muttered, "I don't think he *knows* a lot of Druida City."

The kitten ignored him.

Since Barton seemed calmer about this than she, Enata matched his pace, and regulated her breathing to his. Within half a septhour they stood in the center of a grassy clearing dotted with wildflowers.

Greetings to you, lady! Glabra warbled.

And to you, Glabra, responded a voice so melodious it brought tears of awe to Enata's eyes. She glanced at Barton, who'd stiffened. Resup's eyes looked wide and wild.

"Greetyou," Enata said to the being who materialized before her, a woman with long, deep green and blue streaked hair, voluptuous and gorgeous, wearing pale green draperies. Her skin was golden, her features symmetrical and fine, her eyes midnight blue with an oblong pupil. About her the atmosphere coalesced like the center of a storm, and all the scents of the island sharpened, inundating Enata.

Greetyou, City Librarian, said Celta. *We have much to discuss.*

≈ Chapter 23 ≈

What would you ask of me first, PublicLibrarian of the City of Druida, Celta, Enata Losa Licorice? I have found that you Licorices are curious, and you demonstrate that.

Enata blurted the first question that surfaced. "This amazing place has birds and animals I've never seen or even imagined."

Gesturing gracefully, Celta explained, *The island has several ecosystems. I have a selection of beings from all of my continents, including some of the most fragile. I know the history of your original planet, that which you call Earth, and how you humans destroyed some beings. That will not be allowed here.*

Enata swallowed her protest. Before she formed her next question, Barton pulled her over to flat slab of rock, perfect for them to sit side by side and study the female avatar.

Ask something more personal. "How do you know so much about me?"

When you are here on the island, I can sift through your memories while you sleep. I know all that any of my folk know, or have learned. I know what sent your ancestors running from that ancient Earth.

Enata's stomach clutched and Barton swore. She put a hand on his thigh to soothe them both. Resup had deserted them to chase flutterbys—that the planet provided for his amusement?—in the glade.

A notion occurred to Enata. Celta now knew everything she did of *Lugh's Spear*.

She heard the laughter of a frolicking breeze through wind chimes, the woman's smile broke like the most exquisite dawn. *As if I didn't know where any of those three space vehicles of you humans landed! As if I didn't take Lugh's Spear into myself to study it.*

Enata valiantly suppressed a surge of anger. Celta had claimed lives when the ground had collapsed under the starship so long ago. Words spurted from her mouth, anyway. *Is all of our history shaped by you?*

But no! I have little to do with any of the sicknesses or diseases that sweep through my atmosphere and affect you. A thoughtful hum as she tapped lush lips with an elegant finger. *Though I suppose I could study them and modify them.*

Please, don't interfere with us! Enata exclaimed.

The ground shifted under their rock, and only there, extremely localized. Barton steadied her. His darkened expression included a clenched jaw.

Not even if I interfere for good? asked Celta.

Some tone warned Enata to treat this being as if she were . . . well, she *was* a goddess.

I have modified weather and winters for you puny humans.

And we thank you. But we wish to—ah, 'make our mark on this world' certainly wasn't the right phrasing—*determine our own destiny.*

Now the planet's voice came cool and crackling, like that icy winter, her eyes deepened to the blackness of space. *I have interfered minimally. I will not change my jetstreams or any weather if it might devastate those of my own, the beasts and birds and plants I shelter and love.* A thoughtful pause. *I will not say that you humans wouldn't have survived without my help, but there would only be small colonies of you at the original sites of the places you call Druida City and Chinju. You would not have had the numbers to expand from them. And I would not have begun to collect and shelter my own humans here on Cyfrinach if I did not want you human animals to thrive.*

Enata let out a breath and walked to the middle of the glen and curtseyed deeply to the planet—the woman's voice in her head and the vision before her who *wasn't* the Lady whom Enata worshipped. She had to remember that. This one had no equal spouse and partner. A huge shaft of pain at the thought of such loneliness speared her. The remembrance of such loneliness.

Barton joined her.

Celta sighed like a massive stream of wind, her clothing fluttering. *It is good to have other minds to speak with . . . not EQUAL minds, but intelligent beings with other perspectives.*

Barton brushed his fingers against Enata's hand, but didn't take it. She felt the wariness of the fight in him.

Barton wanted his say. He glanced around and flourished a bow as if to the highest in all of Celta, definitely not meeting those strange eyes. "Lady, I would speak to you about taking the memories of the Chosen from their Family members."

The more who remember, the more chance it is that my people on my island will be interfered with. That I, myself, might be discovered and I am not one who wishes to be worshipped or prayed to or expected to grant trivial boons.

"Let Enata be a judge of who can know and who can't," Barton persuaded. "You have observed generations of Licorice Librarians. Have any betrayed you, even bent their word to you, their vows?"

I will consider. I have a very good and gentle link with your waking minds now. You may leave this place.

So he and Enata walked in silence—punctuated by Resup's squeals as he chased leaves and twigs rolled by the breeze and pounced, Glabra's ever cheerful melody. They'd reached the point on the cliffs to look out over the bay and the *Lady of Celta* that readied for the next voyage to Druida City, and watched that for some minutes, before Celta spoke again. This time she didn't materialize.

I will allow the current Librarian embedded in the human culture, Enata Losa Licorice, to call upon me to lift the mists of ignorance from certain human brains. But there will be a price, always, to those who demand to remember bonds to the Chosen or wish to know of my presence.

"A price," Barton said warily.

Much like the one you and the Librarian have paid. If I have not met the person, that individual must come to this island to make herself or himself known to me that I might observe him and her and judge them worthy of their knowledge.

"The headaches and sickness," Enata murmured. "The disruption of our natural rhythms as experienced by others."

"The bad vibrations," Barton added.

"*But,*" Enata said in tones of steel, "*you must not*

take away Balansa's memories of her brother when she leaves with us."

Unacceptable, Celta said. *She is a sub-adult and cannot be trusted to be quiet.*

"Yes, she can." Enata set her feet in the rock, ready to take a stand and fight. Barton had never admired her more.

"You cannot rip the entire memory of her brother away from her. You will break her." Enata's chin set. "And no matter how many people, *sentient beings* you've hurt and broken in the past"

"Including Enata," Barton added. "Including Reglis who even now is upset because none of his Family remembers his existence."

"—I believe you are a compassionate person, and will not deliberately hurt people in the future. It's not what a decent being does."

Barton heard Enata inhale, then watched as she gracefully slid down to sit, and placed her hands on the ground. "Hear me, Lady Celta. Listen. I give you permission to deeply review my emotions and see how your tampering with my memories and the memories of my Family, removing Reglis from our recollections, harmed us!"

Horrified, Barton surged forward, slammed into an invisible spellshield and bounced back hard, landing on his ass. There he could only wait and watch, and pant with fear.

FamMan needs me! Resup darted out of the bushes and onto his lap. Barton picked his Fam up in both hands, liking the softness of the baby fur, the couple of licks Resup gave him.

FamWoman needs me! The bird succeeded

where Barton couldn't and flew to Enata. *I will sit on her head! I will keep her head good!*

Barton fervently hoped so. In fact, he prayed to the Lady and Lord of his religion. And he sat and petted his Fam and watched as his beloved turned pale and trembled as an unimaginable entity played with her mind. He breathed and counted his breaths in and out to a hundred. Stopped and counted again. A third time, a fourth, and he lost track after that, except he knew the sun changed its angle and Resup fell asleep purring.

Finally Enata slumped.

Barton carefully tipped Resup from his shaking hands, leapt to his feet, went over to Enata and yanked her upright against him. And began to spew his fear. "You damn well should not have done that, Enata, and especially not by yourself, and not without consulting me."

"So-rry," she whispered.

"You should be," he said. His throat hurt. As if he'd been yelling all the while out loud instead of screaming silently.

You should be, echoed Resup. *You scared us bad!* The kitten clawed up Barton's trous leg and then his sleeve to anchor himself on Barton's shoulder.

"Sorry."

"You damn well talk to me before you do anything that might drive you mad or kill you. I mean it, Enata."

"I apologize," she said, her voice muffled against his chest. Then she cleared her throat. "I will ask the same of you."

"I agree," he said. "But you're indebted to me for

one fliggering heart-stopping scare. You damn well remember that."

"All right."

"And I'm still angry with you."

"All right." She paused, and he realized he wasn't the only one shaking, she did, too. They just sort of shook in unison.

After about a quarter septhour, they'd settled, their hearts now beating together and in a regular, steady rhythm.

Before they left the ridge, Celta spoke,

I state my conclusions as follows: First: I see that removing all knowledge of her brother Savi will permanently maim the sub-adult Balansa, so I have allowed her to keep her memories. I have placed a silence spell upon Balansa so that she cannot speak of her brother to anyone except the City Librarian. Balansa's recollections of other Chosen and the island will fade. Second: The City Librarian's mate's memories will also fade. Third: All of the City Librarian's memories will remain intact. I have given the City Librarian the means to allow remembrance of me and any Chosen I have already taken to individuals she believes should be informed. I emphasize that there will be a price to be paid for such knowledge. Fourth and finally, I am reconsidering my policies of removing all memories of my Chosen from their Family members after understanding the ramifications of such distress upon the Licorice, Hazel, Heather, Mor, and Vine Families from facts I found in the City Librarian's memories of these Families. I will also consider modifying my qualifications of Chosen to include affect on Families if memories were excised, but I will decide who retains memories and who does not upon a case by case basis. Those are my conclusions. You may leave the island at your convenience.

"We thank you," Barton forced himself to say, yanked the *feeling* of gratitude from his depths and projected it to the great being of Celta. He bowed in the four directions.

"We thank you," Enata said, curtseying in each direction.

Thanks, Celta! Resup said. *I want to go back to Druida City that's more interesting!*

Thank you, lady, sang Glabra. *I know you will be with me as we sing together, but I am pleased to go with my FamWoman.*

≈ Chapter 24 ≈

That evening they told Reglis and Captain Mor that they'd be ready to depart for Druida City the next day at MidMorning Bell. When night fell both Resup and Glabra deserted them—Resup to help Glabra gather things from here to take for a nest she'd establish in Druida City.

Enata had taken a waterfall with Barton and he'd displayed excellent skill in pleasuring them both. Now she sat wrapped in a thin silkeen robe and watched Barton, who only wore a towel around his waist, obtain a couple of flutes of prime fizz wine from the no-time. His every movement was efficient and virile.

There was no sexier man in the world than Barton Clover.

She stilled as dread washed through her bringing a rush of horrible questions. *Could* someone have read her mind and provided this man? More, could have bespelled both of them to love at first sight?

The same, powerful person, powerful force who'd erased the memories of the lost family members. Celta.

Did that entity manipulate human emotions? Mold them to fit with another's?

The deep horror of it caught Enata's breath. Exactly how much might have the planet controlled her . . . and Barton. Was their love real? And if not, would they fall *out of love* at some point in the future? How terrible!

Barton stood in front of her, frowning. He placed both glasses on a side table, picked her from her chair, sat, and put her on his lap. "What's wrong?"

Since she panted and could feel his concern, so he must be feeling her panic, she couldn't deny anything.

"Best tell me about it." He wrapped his arms around her, and even naked from he waist up, he kept her warm.

"I had a few thoughts."

"Okay, tell me."

"The planet made us love each other, not normal falling in love or love at first sight." She gulped, calculated. "It all started at the dark of the twinmoons, the first day of the month of Reed."

He stroked her hair. "I had my appointment with the matchmaker before the dark of the twinmoons, the last week of the month of Ivy."

She relaxed, but her mind kept running. "And when did your quest truly begin?"

He froze. "The disappearances occurred at Ivy full twinmoons."

Tears coated her throat, backed up, stinging, behind her eyes. "Both potent twinmoons cycles. We've been manipulated."

"Let's ask the planet." A sharp smile edged his lips, and he squeezed her. "But I'm not giving you up."

She bit her lip, swallowed hard. "I don't like thinking we've been bespelled. What happens if the spell wears off? I couldn't bear it. Better that we end our relationship now, when the hurt won't—"

"The hurt now would fliggering tear me apart. And how the fligger do you think we'd live? And what about children for our Families? You're not leaving me again. We made vows, Enata."

"You're right. I'm running scared. Again."

Barton pointed to the luxurious square carpet that had a circular floral border and the four directions picked out with woven bouquets. "We'll just stand right there in that circle and ask Celta." He set her on her feet, and when he took his place, he stood braced as if for a fight.

He took her hand and put it over his heart. "We marry for love, we Clovers. So far. We haven't been noble enough for us to get any ideas that we should increase our status or fortune or whatever—" he stopped. "Well, Walker had a problem with the elders, but he resolved that in his usual quiet Walker fashion."

"I'm sure his HeartMate Sedwy had something to say about it."

Barton grinned. "Yes, she did."

Seeing him smile unwound the tension enveloping Enata.

With a jerk of his chin, he asked aloud, "So, Celta, we call on you for information. Have you manipulated me and Enata to fall in love with each other?"

Why is it important that I fashioned you for each other in your mothers' wombs?

Barton sat abruptly on the carpet, pulling Enata down with him.

"Because we prefer to find our own destiny?" Enata squeaked, trying to get her mind around the new information.

The whole room seemed to waver in her vision and Barton rocked against her.

You do not understand the dynamics of the universe, Celta said. *You love and are loved. That is sufficient.*

"Do you also do HeartMates and HeartBonds?" Enata asked.

No, those are beyond Me. Created by a greater power.

"Lady and Lord," Enata whispered.

"Lord and Lady," Barton said gruffly, at the same time. He fell backward and took her with him. They lay there, on the thick patterned rugs like nothing they'd seen before, staring up at the beautiful patterned wood above them, for long minutes.

Finally Barton cleared his throat. "I think I can accept that I've been manipulated by our planet, our home, to love you, to fit with you."

"Me too," Enata said inelegantly.

"All right, then."

Their eyes met. She took his hand and led him to the bedsponge. There she made love to him tenderly, thoroughly, hoping the love she felt for him wasn't artificial, wouldn't fade.

But a shard of fear that unnatural love could vanish lodged in her heart. She wished they'd been HeartMates.

≈ Chapter 25 ≈

Midmorning the next day, Captain Mor stood stiff and straight near the end of the gangplank that led up to the ship, *The Lady of Celta.* Enata, Barton, Balansa and the Fams awaited the signal to board.

After one last hug, Reglis snapped his fingers and translocated a box. "For you and Barton. Please open them now."

Enata unwrapped the gift, tucking bow and paper into one of her sleeves, Barton took off the top of the box and pushed back softleaves to reveal gorgeous marriage armbands. Lined with bespelled velvet, the base was copper, and the engraved panels pure gold. The etching showed eternal Celtic marriage knots framed by a clover blossom on one side and a spray of licorice leaves on the other.

"I noticed you didn't wear marriage armbands," Reglis said.

"We married quickly," Barton said gruffly. "Didn't pick any out. These are fabulous. We'll treasure them."

"Such a wonderful gift!" She flung herself against her brother and squeezed him hard, was glad of his tight clasp.

When he let go, he blinked several times. "Don't be a stranger. Come back now and again. You can, you know."

"I know. I might." She glanced at Barton. They all knew his memory of this would fade.

Barton shrugged. "I'll probably go off on training missions now and then, you can come here."

Reglis slapped him on the shoulder. "Barton, you

are a man among men."

"I know."

"And now we're linked again, we can speak telepathically," Reglis said. He closed his eyes a few seconds. "You can keep me up to date on the Family."

"And everything else," Enata added.

Eyes damp, Reglis turned to Balansa and said, "I have a gift for you, too." Another snap of his fingers and a small black and white kitten appeared in his hands.

Her shriek of happiness bounced off the cliffs of the bay, mingling with the kitten's plaintive mews and Resup's demands to *See a new Fam friend!*

With a grimace, Captain Mor stepped up and snapped another tiny orange vest around the kitten.

Then last hugs around and they trooped up the gangplank.

Barton helped the crew raise the platform and stow it, then looked toward where he last saw Reglis. The man had vanished, teleporting to the Castle, though Barton would bet any amount of gilt that Reglis would be watching from a tower until *The Lady of Celta* sailed out of sight. A good man, and one who loved his job as much as Enata did hers. This separation was tough on the both of them. Enata had already disappeared below, not wanting to see the island that held her brother diminish in the distance.

Turning to the Captain, Barton said, "I thank you for bringing us here and taking us back."

"Just doing my job," Mor said.

Barton shrugged. "Is there anything I can do for *you*?"

The Captain measured him with wary eyes. After a couple of breaths, he said, "I'd like a membership to The Green Knight Fencing and Fighting Salon. Like to go there on shore leave in Druida City."

"I can do that," Barton said. If he couldn't get the Hollys to donate a membership, he and the Clovers could buy one for the Captain. Always good to have an influential acquaintance. And as *the* physical connection between Druida City and Cyfrinach Island, Captain Mor was a good acquaintance to have.

Reaching into his jacket pocket, Mor handed a piece of papyrus and a writestick to Barton. "Better write down a promissory scrip for that membership for me. 'Cuz you'll be forgetting all about it in a little while."

Barton wrote: *I hereby promise Captain Mor—*

"Spell it 'Moores'," the Captain instructed.

Doing so, Barton finished the note and handed back to Mor, along with the writestick. "When will my memory start to fail?"

"Once we pass the halfway point from the island to the peninsula. Good luck to you."

"And to you." Barton tried a smile, but it turned lopsided. "I won't remember you when you introduce yourself to me in Druida City and remind me of the note, but . . . maybe we can build an acquaintance there."

For once the man's eyes didn't look like hard marbles. He dipped his head. "Maybe."

* * *

The first part of the trip passed well, if with a touch of melancholy. When they reached the midpoint, Barton came down with a fever for several septhours, then moaned, shuddered once, and fell into a deep sleep. When he awoke, he had no knowledge of Savi or the events on Cyfrinach Island other than their sexual bouts and that Enata had claimed a new FamCompanion.

As she'd promised before they left, Enata told him he was missing memories, and that he could have them back, but the price would be steep. Since he *did* recall her suffering in the vault, if not the cause, he grunted but didn't press her. As time wore on, his mood lightened as he played with Balansa, the kitten, and talked to Glabra about the best things to have in a nest-home.

Until a septhour before they reached Druida City.

* * *

"Something's wrong," Barton muttered. He'd come up to stand next to Enata and look over the rail in the direction of Druida City.

"What?" she asked.

He rubbed his neck, then his chest. "Something is definitely wrong." Lifting his face into the breeze coming from the distant shore, he inhaled. Then he rubbed over his heart. "It's Walker."

"Walker?"

"Walker's sick." Barton turned to her, glowering. "These damn memories that I've lost. Is there something in them that might have affected Walker, too? Hurt him?"

Dismay filled her, but she'd promised to answer any of his questions honestly. "Perhaps."

"Cave of the Dark Goddess!" He banged the rail of the ship with his fist, then muttered more vile curses she hadn't heard him use before. He swung around. "Captain Mor, can we go any faster?" he shouted.

The Captain strode up to them with his rolling walk and face set in hard lines. "Maybe. If I think we should." He looked at Enata.

"How sick is Walker?" she asked.

"Sick enough."

So she nodded to Captain Mor. "I think that if we can get more speed, we should." Curving her mouth in a small smile, she said, "And the sooner we land, the sooner you're rid of us."

"There is that," the Captain grunted. He stalked away, gathered some of his crew around him and they went to the prow. Enata sensed great Flair, and a touch of that *otherness,* planetary energy, and the ship picked up significant speed.

As soon as they'd docked, they heard a yell, "Barton! Barton Clover, are you there?"

"Yes!" Barton shouted back.

When they disembarked, two of Barton's guards ran up to them, linked her and Balansa—whom they'd recognized—and Barton together and teleported them to Clover Compound.

≈ Chapter 26 ≈

They alit outside Walker's chambers, Balansa shaky with weariness. Thankfully, Resup slept in the duffle and Glabra sat quiet and fluffed on Enata's shoulder.

One of the older women took Balansa away to sleep with Trif Clover Winterberry's family, and Barton strode into Walker's bedroom, drawing Enata with him.

The Head of the Household looked bad. Worse off than Barton had been when he'd lost his memory, awake but weak. Barton politely asked Walker's HeartMate to go for clucker soup and dark bread and after one long stare, she'd agreed.

Barton glared at Enata, widened his stance, and crossed his arms.

"We're suffering from memory loss," he informed his brother. "Enata, as a PublicLibrarian, has the information, but I have refrained from asking her about it. Until now.

"I think we should know."

"Know what?" Enata delayed.

"Everything," both men said in unison.

Raising her brows, she faced off against the two Clovers. "I would advise against this."

"We need to know."

"Why?" She truly thought that the worst was over for them. Obviously they both had been tied to Savi as a distant cuz, but from what Barton had told her before, they barely knew him. "You need to know because you are the Head of the Household and Chief of Security for a large Family." She shrugged. "I'm sure you have secrets, even Family secrets I will never be told. We, the Licorices, have and protect secrets, too. Let this one be."

Barton stood even taller. "Walker will someday be the most powerful man on Celta, the Captain of All the Councils."

She *had* heard that. "To me that's more of a reason for him *not* to know."

Both Clover brows wrinkled in frustration.

"Walker would never abuse power."

Walker angled to a straighter position and even that effort seemed to cost him. "Whatever happened is hurting me, and through me, my Family." He rubbed his chest. "It's limiting my ability to protect them. And if the effects linger, or occur again. . ." He shook his head. "I don't want my Family hurt."

She stared at the two stubborn men for a full minute, and her own will began to weaken. So much easier to be with Barton without this particular secret between them.

If Walker knew of Celta and the Chosen, she might be able to ask him for advice. She believed other Clovers would be Chosen in the future. Wetting her lips, she repeated, "There will be a physical price to pay for this knowledge."

"We will pay it," Walker stated, white around the mouth.

It only took a wisp of a thought of Celta, the first Word of the long spell rhyme the entity had taught her, for Enata to feel the deep interest of the being who was a planet. And pause.

"No," she said, looking at the half-brothers. "No. I'm not going to tell you." Glabra shifted on Enata's shoulder, but said nothing.

"I am the head of the Family," Walker stated, and she felt his Flair fill the room. A touch of charisma, but most of all, empathy—and . . . at that minute he removed the dulling shields of all the threads of the individual Clover bonds. All the ties he had, Barton had, to the nearly two hundred member Family.

She made a sound as they began to twine through her and Barton hesitated, but came to her and put a hand on her shoulder. That helped her deal with the influx of emotional ties. In the shadows of all the other links, she felt the one that only she and Balansa knew of—Savi.

Stiffening her spine, she stood solid and nodded once to Walker. "You are the head of the Clover Family, but not the Licorices, and head of the Family or not, every person must decide the points of their own honor and to act responsibly."

Barton dropped his hand from her shoulder, and that hurt, hurt. Her mouth dry, she continued. "For your protection, and the protection of all the Clovers and, in fact, the protection of us all, I am not going to tell you."

Walker appeared offended, but wary. Anger slipped from Barton to her along the bond.

"You're judging me?" Walker asked.

Again a dark stirring of a tendril of the lady of Celta. "One of the prices for you to pay is a journey like the one Barton and I made." Anxiety, trying to do the right thing for everyone, made her smile sharp. "An open-ended journey." She put up her hand and stroked Glabra with the backs of her fingers. "It could be trying. Would you go, Walker

Clover? Alone, or take your HeartMate and children? Some . . . rituals demand days. Can you afford days away from Druida City?"

Walker crossed his arms. "I don't like your tone."

"I don't like your demands." She looked at him, watched Barton from the corner of her eye. "And if you don't respect me and my judgment, now, when you are *not* the most powerful man on Celta, will you make even more demands of those around you when you are? Listen only to your wants and needs at the expense of others?"

"We're protecting the Family," Barton said in a rough voice.

"Are you? By hurting one member of the Family? Me?" She took in an uneven breath. "There are truisms that apply here. 'Absolute power corrupts absolutely.' 'The ends justify the means.' I won't tell you this particular secret."

"You may go then," Walker said. "Barton, I'd like to debrief you on everything." Walker waved and the door opened.

Not looking at Barton, but with a cooing Glabra cradled in her hands, she left.

Would Barton follow her? Choose her over his Family? She didn't know, and sometime in the last few minutes, their bond had closed to a strand. She took the wide marble stairs down, walked slowly along the wide hallway to a door she thought open into the courtyard. One of the three courtyards of the long blocks of Clover Compound.

Despite the continuing discomfort of all the bonds of all the people pushing at her, despite

Walker seeming to give her a choice between her Family or the Clovers, Enata would stay. Somehow she would find Barton's home. It had been on the east . . .

Now that she truly felt the links of the Clover Family, among some individuals was a dark trauma of missing Savi.

And she realized that love would get them through, heal those fractures in the Family when one went missing. Only love could do that. Her Family had been mending, and she'd work hard on ensuring her sister and her parents knew she loved them, on weaving the bonds between them all—love bonds—tighter.

Love had to be the only way such wounds could heal. She would also observe the Hazels, the Heathers, and the Mors. Perhaps invite them to certain rituals. She knew a creative priestess who crafted good rituals for specific purposes.

Then, no more than half way down the courtyard, strong arms grabbed her from behind, and swung her up against a broad chest. Glabra chirped in happy welcome and transferred to Barton's shoulder.

"You chose me." Enata's voice trembled.

"I will always choose you," he murmured near her ear, stirring her hair.

"Even over your Family."

"You are my Family." His breath came a little rough. "I admit I like to be in control, and am overprotective. But I've learned that I can't hold myself responsible for everything that happens to a member of my Family. And that my life should be more than working to keep them safe. I have you now." He tightened his grip around her, then swung her to her feet and twined his fingers with hers.

"So you told Walker, what?"

"That I trust you. That you're my wife and if he doesn't trust you, then I can resign and head up security for the Licorice clan."

The shock had her jerking. "You did?"

"I did. He was pleased, and when his HeartMate returned, she was pleased, too. I translocated my duffle and Resup home." He glanced at Glabra. "I've got my woman now. Why don't you fly and explore the Compound?"

She flicked her tail, chirped mentally, *I am happy to do so!* and took off.

Barton continued, "Oh, and Walker said that if you think the FirstFamily nobles will ever let him have absolute power, you should think again."

"There is that." She rubbed her head, but now felt the flicker of attention she'd had from Celta was gone. Then Enata brought up something bothering her. "We aren't HeartMates."

"I'm glad you're not my HeartMate," Barton squeezed her. "Should I die, our children will not be abandoned by both parents. Even with all the Clovers to help them, my brothers and sisters and nieces and nephews, I don't want that."

Enata's voice clogged with horrified tears. "I don't think I could go on well without you, HeartMate or not."

He pivoted fast, lifted her chin so she met his intense gaze. "You would not abandon our young children."

Gulping, she shook her head. "No. But though my body might not die, I think my heart would." Again she shook her head in denial. "I can't think of that. Please don't make me think of that. We will grow old and die together in bed." She said it like a spell, hoped the entity of Celta listened.

Barton's lips quirked. "Having sex."

She closed her eyes at the embarrassment of that particular scenario.

"We wouldn't be around to be humiliated," he pointed out, issuing her through the doors of the wing between two of the Clover Compound blocks.

They traversed the short corridor in silence. As they reached the door to the next courtyard, Enata saw through the window that the area was populated. This was the original square of houses built by the Clovers, the main outside living space of Clover Compound.

≈ Chapter 27 ≈

She tugged Barton to stop. "What would you say if I told you we were made for each other?"

He promptly lifted her hand to his lips. "I'd say I knew it all along."

But she had to know, had to *feel,* had to probe to his farthest depths, and her own, to vanquish that last fear that this sudden love would evaporate. She turned and put her hands on his shoulders, looked into his eyes, and opened herself as she hadn't since she'd drunk the potion at T'Willow's.

Her mind spun together with his, her emotions mingled with his and she plunged down, down, down into her own heart and found the sparkling wonder and solid belief in him, as her one and only true love. When she peered as deeply into him, she saw the same reflected.

Enough, for now.

He kissed the top of her head. "My dear wife."

"Yes."

Then he pushed open the door and nodded as people greeted them. They angled across the courtyard to a large, refurbished looking house.

"We've moved?"

"You like the afternoon, western sun in the windows, and looking out in the direction of the ocean." He studied the building and nodded. "It's very well situated, security-wise."

On one of the eaves, Glabra warbled. *I have found a perfect place for a nest! Resup is sleeping in the kitchen!*

"Thank you," they said in unison.

Barton turned to her and clasped her other hand. "'*Come live with me and be my love, And we will all the pleasures prove, That valleys, groves, hills and fields, Woods or steepy mountains yield.*'"

Her brows rose. "I know a rebuttal for that."

He touched her lips. "So do I, but don't say it."

She kissed his fingers, even touched them with her tongue and he jerked his hand back, gave her a hot look.

Her own voice husky, she said, "*Come live with me and be my love, And we will all the pleasures prove . . .*"

Again he acted, sweeping her into his arms. "Door open!" he ordered. The dark brown wooden door opened outward and Barton strode in. Pale beige-cinnamon walls welcomed them along with the scent of the Clover Family, and Barton.

"Close door," he murmured, staring down on her with such a look of tenderness she was glad he held her because her muscles had weakened and her core gone molten, needing him.

"We will *all* the pleasures prove since you have come to live with me . . ."

"And you are my love," they said in unison, gazes locked.

The End

Author's Notes

If you enjoyed this novella, please leave a review on the online site of your choice. This is my first venture into self-publishing and I really appreciate all the support you can give me.

This novella sprang from several cut scenes from the novel *Heart Fortune*. Those scenes were in the viewpoint of Glyssa Licorice (Enata's sister) and Jace Bayrum (Glyssa's HeartMate). I have posted the scenes on my blog (you may have to do a search for them).

Throughout the series I misplaced a few people (the Hazel-Heather couple and Enata's older brother), and I wanted to address this, as well as throw a twist into the series, which is why this novella was written.

Since I am accustomed to writing longer books (more than twice as long as *Lost Heart*), I also cut scenes from this novella: a couple from the beginning, a couple from after Enata left the Clover Compound, Enata's meeting with the Castle Healer, and one near the end.

Acknowledgments:

Michelle Kaye and Samantha States who helped me with the print copy! And the fabulous Rose Beetem who did my line and copy edits!

About the Author

RITA® Award-winning author Robin D. Owens has been writing longer than she cares to recall. Her fantasy/futuristic romances found a home at Berkley with the issuance of *HeartMate* in December 2001. She credits the "telepathic cat with attitude" in selling that book. Currently, she has two domesticated cats (who have appeared in her stories).

She loves writing fantasy with romance or romance with fantasy, and particularly likes adding quirky characters for comic relief and leaving little threads dangling from book to book to see if readers pick up on them (usually, yes! Reader intelligence is awesome!).

Robin loves hearing from readers, tries her best to respond to any questions and has been known to take reader advice for her work (e.g. the mole in *Heart Thief*). Please email her at robindowens@gmail.com

She also spends (too much) time on Facebook and will answer questions there:

https://www.facebook.com/robin.d.owens.73

She is profoundly thankful to be a recipient of the 2002 Romance Writers of America RITA® Award (like the Oscar in her field) for *HeartMate,* and various other awards.

When she receives good reviews or fan mail, she's been known to dance around bored cats . . .

Also by Robin D. Owens

Celta HeartMate Series, in Reading Order

**Heart And Sword (story collection *Hearts and Swords*; this first story, *Heart and Sword*, takes place on board the generational starship *Nuada's Sword*)

HeartMate
Heart Thief
Heart Duel
Heart Choice
Heart Quest
Heart Dance
**HeartStory (story collection, *Hearts and Swords Story*)
Heart Fate
**Heart and Soul (story collection, *Hearts and Swords*)
Heart Change
***Zanth and the Treasure (free short, short story, available online)
Heart Journey
***Script of the Heart novella, coming Autumn 2016
**Noble Heart (story collection, *Hearts and Swords*)
Heart Search
Heart Secret
Heart Fortune (Glyssa Licorice and Jace Bayrum)
Lost Heart (this novella!)
Heart Fire
Heart Legacy
Heart Sight (coming 2017)

* * *

The Ghost Series (contemporary paranormal)

Ghost Seer
Ghost Layer
Ghost Talker
Ghost Maker (coming October 2016)

* * *

Feral Magic, a contemporary paranormal romance e-novella

* * *

The Mystic Circle Series
(contemporary fantasy)

Enchanted No More
Enchanted Again
Enchanted Ever After

The Summoning Series

Average American women are summoned to another dimension to fight hideous evil. . .yes, with flying horses!

Guardian of Honor
Sorceress of Faith
Protector of the Flight
Keepers of the Flame
Echoes In the Dark

Reader's Notes

JAN

Made in the USA
Charleston, SC
27 August 2016